Knox Warrior

Discovery Isles

S. E. Amaya

Knox Warrior: Discovery Isles
Copyright © 2021 S. E. Amaya
All rights reserved.

No part of this book may be reproduced in any manner whatsoever without the prior written permission of the publisher, except in the case of brief quotations embodied in reviews.

The views and opinions expressed in this book
are those of the author and do not necessarily reflect
the official policy or position of Halo Publishing International.
Any content provided by our authors are of their opinion and
are not intended to malign any religion, ethnic group, club,
organization, company, individual or anyone or anything.

ISBN: 978-1-61244-952-4
LCCN: 2020924601

Halo Publishing International, LLC
8000 W Interstate 10, Suite 600
San Antonio, Texas 78230
www.halopublishing.com

Printed and bound in the United States of America

This book is dedicated to all dreamers in the world today, no matter how old they may be. There is no greater creative power than that of one's own imagination, so dream big and reach for the impossible, as the word "impossible" has "I'm possible" in it. Believe it and achieve it.

Contents

Introduction	9
Character Profiles	11
CHAPTER ONE Sterling Krystalline	17
CHAPTER TWO Isla Mordaz	53
CHAPTER THREE Python Cove	97
CHAPTER FOUR Skerry Moor	109
CHAPTER FIVE Return to Isla Mordaz	117
CHAPTER SIX Isle of the Ikkakkujuu	139
CHAPTER SEVEN Revisiting Familiar Places	157

Chapter Eight Shark Skull Island	171
Chapter Nine Isla Ellura	189
Chapter Ten The Battle	211
Acknowledgements	237

Introduction

When I entered my first year of high school, I created a bucket list. For those of you who are asking, "What on earth is that?" it is a list of places you want to go to and things you want to do at some point in your lifetime. Two of the locations on my bucket list were London and Ireland. I had always been fascinated with both the Irish culture and the United Kingdom, partly because I was a huge fan of *Harry Potter* when I was growing up. As I reviewed the list I had created, I began to mark off locations, starting back in 2016, when I took my first—and only, so far—trip to Orlando, Florida, to experience the magic of Walt Disney World Resort. I fell in love with Animal Kingdom and came back ready to take more adventures to places on my list. In July of 2020, I took a trip to Seattle, Washington, and was blown away by the beauty and magic of nature. After getting back from Washington, I began to plan for another trip, which I hope to take in March of 2021. "Where?" you may be asking. Oregon, Washington's neighboring state.

Although I have yet to visit the United Kingdom, it has always been a dream of mine to do so, and I hope that I will have the privilege of going soon. While I could not physically visit the United Kingdom during the time I wrote this book, the book was still strongly influenced by Britain and the British Isles. When I was younger, I constantly daydreamed about what it would be like to visit, and in my head I imagined it as something like this book.

The only real-life characters I used—and I got consent to write about them—were my two dogs, Amber and Kobe. Kobe is nine, and Amber is seven. I love them both very much.

I hope that this book will take you on a remarkable adventure of your own and will help you create your own bucket list of things to do and places to see.

Character Profiles

*() signify ages

Main Characters
  Princess: Harper Jane Knox (27)

  King: Henry Knox

  Queen: Skylar Knox

  Royal Aunt: Arwen Kingsly

  Royal Uncle: Tanner Kingsly

  Royal Cousin: Kelsey Kingsly (26)

Swedish Royals
  King: Niall Woods

  Queen: Jade Woods

  Prince: Kellan Maverick Woods (28)

Ships
  Black Mist

  Autumn Corpse

Pirates
  Black Mist Crew:

Captain Kyle Dawson (22)

Mr. Nomad (30)

Kendall Jenkins/Pirate Fairy (24/immortal)

Austin Parker (26)

Bruce Emery (20)

Barton Emery (20)

Prince Kellan Woods (27)

Autumn Corpse Crew:

Captain Hamish Connors (23)

Blaze Park (24)

Keaton Stone (27)

Lola Lawrence (28)

Garret Vons (26)

Vince Perry (29)

Vick Watson (30)

Other Characters

Spencer: Kelsey's best friend (26)

Kobe: pet dog

Shadow: pet dog

Amber: pet dog

Warlock/Raven Claw: Corbin, King Henry's advisor and nephew (29)

Cosmo: Corbin's pet snake

Dash-ren: killer whale/orca

Witches: Clementine and Belinda (best friends) (29)

Winged Fairies: Elle and Will (both 30)

Fairy (non-winged): Heidi and Holly (both 22)

Warlock: Lennox (26)

Dinosaurs

Brachiosaurus

Iguanodon

Pterodactyl

Triceratops

Spinosaurus

Velociraptor

Dilophosaurus

Parasaurolophus

Tyrannosaurus Rex

Stegosaurus

Quetzalcoatlus Northropi (half huge Pelecan, half Pterodactyl [bottom half] mix)

Ceratosaurus

Baryonyx

Carnotaurus

Stygimoloch

Pachycephalosaurus

Ankylosaurus

Pachyrhinosaurus

Merman

Bryce: Harper's best friend, brother of the mermaids listed (28)

Mermaids

Pyra (36)

Leah (34)

Sierra (32)

Violet (30)

Nova (28)

Zoe (26)

Stella (24)

Hilda (22)

Hazel (20)

Other Creatures

Hippocampus

Blue phoenix

Purple phoenix

Gryphon: Hendrix

White peacock

Green peacock

Black-and-navy medusa

Brown-horned dragon

Yellow fire-breathing dragon

Swans

Wolves

Unicorns

Cave spiders

Brown widow spider

Ferret: Jax

Foxes

Wizards

Chapter One

Sterling Krystalline

Once upon a time, in London, England, there lived a king named Henry Knox. King Henry and his family owned acres and acres of land. They lived in a castle made of brick and granite. The palace was called Sterling Krystalline and was well guarded. It resided near the ocean as well as a forest where Princess Harper often loved spending time.

Princess Harper was incredibly beautiful. She had long black hair with bright-blue highlights; it went down to mid-waist on her. She had big brown eyes with long eyelashes. She was about five feet five and looked younger than she was. Aside from beauty, Princess Harper was also incredibly talented and was fond of all music. She loved to sing, write, and dance in her free time. Often, people who visited the palace and heard her singing would tell her that she had the most beautiful voice they had ever heard. Harper enjoyed attending all kinds of concerts and local talent shows while having tea at local coffee or tea houses in the marketplace. She also loved spending hours daydreaming as she picked strawberries, apples, and blueberries in the fields near Sterling Krystalline.

Princess Harper was an only child and spent most of her time going on adventures with her dog, Amber, and her best friend, Bryce. Bryce had come into Harper's life about three months prior, and their friendship was still blossoming. She found herself often questioning why her time with him was limited.

The time Harper and Bryce spent together was always on, or somewhere close to, the beach. A force she could not explain often drew her closer to the sea. There were many times when she dreamed of mermaids and swimming with killer whales. She was very imaginative and yet very rational about things, but her dreams could sometimes warn her of the future. Although her dreams of the sea posed no warning (as far as she knew), some had indeed predicted a piece of the future.

Though she was an only child, Harper lived in the castle with her cousin Corbin. Corbin was two years older than her and had been taken in by Harper's parents when he was a teenager, after they received news that his parents had been killed in a shipwreck. Corbin had asked King Henry if he could have the dungeon as a room, though he had been offered a different room in the castle. After seeing how much Corbin liked the dungeon, and after Corbin showed him his vision for a remodel, King Henry had had it fixed up so it would resemble a bedroom. He had installed a working bathroom, including a shower and a toilet, and because the dungeon was separate from the castle, King Henry had also added a front door that opened to the outside and an inside door that opened into a tunnel leading into the castle.

Corbin was the king's assistant, and he often tried to connect with Harper. Harper was not particularly close with or fond of her cousin. She'd always thought he was mysterious, and she often noticed when he snuck off at night or at weird hours of the day. Still, she thought nothing of it.

Harper was curious, however, about a warlock she encountered one night after having dinner with her parents and Corbin. Corbin ran off like he usually did, but this time Harper decided to follow him. They went down the hallway and out the backdoor of the palace. As she watched him run off into town, she followed him closely, but then he noticed her following him. Corbin ran straight into a group of locals, knocking them down, and Harper lost track of him. After dusting herself off and apologizing to the locals, she walked toward the nearest tavern to use the restroom. Upon entering the tavern, she spotted the warlock. He had on a black and purple cloak that was covered with shimmering silver glitter, and he wore a black eye mask. Harper, drawn by the glitter on his cloak, walked over to his table and ordered a ginger beer.

"What is your name? I love your cloak. Did you make it?" she asked, intrigued.

"My name is Raven Claw. It's a pleasure meeting you, Princess," Corbin replied, with a grin on his face.

Harper, not realizing it was Corbin, was in shock that he knew who she was, and her eyes grew bigger as she asked, "How do you know who I am? And who are you? What is it that you do? What do you want?" she asked.

"Don't be alarmed, Your Highness. I sold garments like the one I am wearing to your father, King Henry, long ago, when you were younger. I mean no harm. I am simply here to get my pet snake some food and water. He's on my lap as we speak," Corbin said, grinning again.

Harper paused and then replied, "Does your pet bite?"

"No, he won't bite people unless I ask him to. He's actually quite cuddly," Corbin said.

"Well, let's see him, then. Does he have a name?" Harper asked with a grin.

"His name is Cosmo," Corbin said.

"Is there a reason you chose that name?" she replied, staring at the ball python in Corbin's lap.

"Yes, do you see his skin? It reminds me of galactic space colors," Corbin said.

"Well, he's beautiful for a snake. He's the perfect shade of blue," she replied.

Harper then looked up and realized she had been gone far too long already, and she needed to head back home. When she turned back around to thank Corbin for their conversation, she saw that he had vanished. There was nothing left but a small card that had *Raven Claw, master of robes and fine linens* written on it. Below that, there was a small photo of a raven in a cloak much like the one he had been wearing that night. She took the card and asked a local for a ride back to Granite Manor, paying the person with silver.

As Princess Harper was arriving at Sterling Krystalline, she heard a cackling caw from a raven that had stooped on a nearby tree outside the castle. She stared at the raven for a moment and thought it was peculiar, especially considering the name that had been on the card, but she soon brushed it off and entered her home through the backdoor, heading down the hall and up the stairs so she could ready herself and her dog, Amber, for bed. As they fell asleep, rain began to fall outside her window, and the cold, crisp air began to sneak in.

***

The next day, before shutting the window, Harper looked out and saw a ship in the distance. It was sitting at the port in Tilbury. Curious, she got ready, fed Amber, and ran down the stairs of the manor, shouting, "I'll be back, Mother. I am going into town and taking the dog. She'll love to get some fresh air in the fields today."

Harper's mother did not respond, as she was trying to fix the binding on some books about legends and myths. The books intrigued her, and she loved looking at the pictures, although she was not too sure she believed everything in them.

The ship that was resting at the port was a pirate ship. It was disguised by magic so that commoners could not see it. It was all black and had green stripes on the inside and outside of it. The mist that surrounded the ship was a green cloud that would show up when the crew was in danger or when there was a change in the weather. The lights on the ship were also green, and the writing on the ship was silver. A skull rested at the bow of the ship, and there was one at the rear. The crew consisted of seven pirates, including their captain. The ship was called the Black Mist.

Aboard the Black Mist was a prince named Kellan. Kellan was the only child of King Niall and Queen Jade, who were from Sweden. When Kellan was just a boy, he had seen a similar ship out at the port near his palace. He had decided to explore the ship that day, but he lost track of time and fell asleep below the deck. After he'd awoken, he'd realized he was in the company of pirates and was aboard a ship called the Black Mist. Captain Kyle Dawson and his crew had taken him in and raised him, though they had been just as surprised to see him aboard their ship.

Captain Dawson's crew consisted of Mr. Nomad, who was a merchant, a sailor, and a respectable man; Austin Parker, Kellan's best friend; the brothers Bruce and Barton Emery; and Kendall Jenkins, a pirate fairy from an island called Encantra. Contrary to popular belief, Kendall was human-sized, and she had special wings that disappeared when necessary. Her wardrobe was full of black and baby-pink glitter. She had the power to set the ship afloat with her pixie dust, which was a mixture of black and purple dust that she kept hidden inside a star-shaped necklace that she wore around her neck. Kendall was married to Austin.

The crew aboard the Black Mist had been at Port Paradise on the island of Encantra before arriving in Tilbury to restock on food and water. They had been searching for a ring. This ring was said to be powerful. It could unleash powers beyond understanding. Previously, other pirates had found it buried on the Isle of Venom, inside a rock formation that resembled the shape of a snake. That place was otherwise known as Python Cove. Legend had it that long before Sterling Krystalline had been built, a wealthy king had stored a chest full of jewels and his crown in that very spot. Pirates had been searching for the treasure for some time. Therefore, it was no mystery that the pirates of Black Mist had greater motives for their visit.

As the pirate's ship was being tied to the port, Harper was in the marketplace. She had disguised herself as a commoner, as she wanted to see what the pirates were up to and why they had come to Port Tilbury to refill, restock, and rest. Although she had gotten awfully close to the pirates, she did not speak to them; she only watched closely from afar, wondering what their motives were.

After she went back to the castle, she changed into her bathing suit and headed to the beach to see Bryce. She told him about the pirates and what she had seen. As they talked, Harper suggested they go shell searching, which was something they usually did, so they did. While they were picking up shells of all shapes and sizes, Bryce suddenly stopped and yelled, "Harper! Come here! Quick! I think I found something unusual."

Harper ran over to where he was, and they both stared at the seashell. The shell was black and medium-sized, and it had blue crystals on the outer parts.

"It's beautiful. Let's have a look inside, shall we? Maybe we'll find a pearl," she said.

When she opened the seashell, to her surprise, there was nothing inside. She closed it and then said to Bryce, "I think we should put it in the water. The crystals are sparkling."

So, they both walked into the ocean, stuck the shell in the water, and opened it. Once opened, a glowing pink magic dust spilled out. Bryce took some of the dust and sprinkled it on Harper. Before she realized what was happening, she turned into a mermaid. She had a black tail covered with silvery-blue seashells, and she could now breathe underwater.

"I'm a mermaid! This shell has powers. I'm going to keep it safe. We can now have adventures together under the sea," said Harper, smiling happily.

"Just don't let it fall into the wrong hands," Bryce replied, smiling.

"Here," Harper replied, handing him the shell. "I want you to keep it safe for me. I wonder how long this will last."

"Maybe a couple of hours," he answered.

As she swam around, Harper began to think about what other powers the shell might have, and she asked, "What happens if we use the shell's magic on you?"

"Me? Okay, I have to tell you something. I guess now is the opportune moment. I do not think that dust will work on me, because I'm already a merman. That is why every time we hang out, it's always in the water. I always want to swim. I doubt it will have an effect on me," Bryce replied.

"You're a merman? Do show me your tail. I've always wanted to see a real mermaid up close. I am so glad you told me. This explains a lot. I promise I will keep your secret. Let's try the dust anyway and see what happens," she said.

"Are you sure that's a good idea?" Bryce replied.

"Trust me. What's the worst that could happen?" she said.

"Okay, I will give it a go," he replied.

Bryce took the magic dust and sprinkled it on his tail. The dust took an immediate effect and turned his tail into human legs. When Harper saw this, she took some more of the dust and sprinkled it on her tail, as well. The dust turned her tail back into human legs, and she swam up to the shore, carrying Bryce in her arms. When they both reached the surface, Bryce was gasping for air.

"Thanks for saving me, Harper," Bryce said, breathing heavily. "I have legs! Can you believe it? Human legs!"

"I wonder how long this will last. You will have to put the shell in a safe place, and we will have to conserve the dust so we do not run out. For now, let's explore the beach," Harper said.

"That sounds like a good idea," Bryce replied.

Harper and Bryce walked and talked, and Harper looked for sea crabs as she dug in the sand. When she looked up, in the distance, she noticed a black X in the sand. As she looked closer, she grew curious and began walking toward it. Just then, her father rode into town on a carriage. One of Harper's servants walked onto the beach and headed toward them. When Harper saw him, she sprinkled dust from the shell onto Bryce's legs.

"Keep the shell safe. I have to go, but I'll be back," Harper said as she ran into the ocean with Bryce.

Bryce shook his head as if to say okay.

When Harper came back up onto shore, her servant was closer to her. She got up, gathered her belongings, and headed toward the servant.

"Your Highness, your presence is needed in the palace. Your mother has something she would like to give you for tonight's ball," the servant said.

"A ball?" Harper asked.

"Yes, Your Majesty, a ball. Your mother will explain everything back at the castle. Your father is waiting for us in town. Should we head back?" the servant asked.

"Yes, very well," Harper said.

As soon as Harper arrived home, her mother rushed over to her and told her about the ball Harper's father had planned for that evening. Harper hurried to her room and started getting ready. When she was done, she went downstairs to help her parents greet guests. Although she was excited about this ball, she couldn't stop thinking about the X on the beach. She felt distracted and kept thinking about how much she needed to tell Bryce. As she pondered, she finally decided she would go back and visit the beach again the next day so she could finish what had been left unfinished. After that decision had been made, she awaited the arrival of Corbin. Although she didn't know if he had confirmed his attendance, she had a feeling he would come. However, she hadn't anticipated pirates showing up as guests, much less Bryce, so she was shocked when both arrived.

"You're here! Wait, oh my gosh, you are here!" she exclaimed. "Let's go upstairs. I have something I made you earlier."

When they got to her room, Harper ran over and hugged Bryce, asking, "How do you have human legs? And why— Actually, how did you get here?"

"I sprinkled some on my legs. I just wanted to see if it would work again. Once I was on land, I heard your father was throwing a ball, so I decided to attend," he said.

"Well, I'm glad you chose to come, but I was about to head back out to the beach. I found something. An X in the sand. It only appears when the sand is wet. I think we should dig up the X and see what we find. We also don't know how long that magic is going to last on you. If it runs out, you won't be able to breathe," she said. "Oh, and before I forget, the pirates are here. Remember that ship I told you I saw earlier today? I think the pirates are part of that ship's crew."

"I remember. So, do you know why they are here? I never thought you would see that ship again, much less meet its crew all in the same day," Bryce said.

"Me either, but we have to find out what they are up to. Come on!" she replied.

They both headed back to the dining room area, where guests had now gathered. Food had been set out for guests to enjoy.

"What exactly are we watching for?" he said.

"I'm not sure. Anything suspicious," she replied.

The two spilt up and watched the pirates from two different areas. Suddenly, Bryce fell to the floor. Harper saw him and ran toward him.

"Oh no, the magic has worn out. We need more, or we have to get you back to the beach now!" Harper said.

Kendall, one of the pirates, had been watching the two from a distance, and she came over to them when she saw what happened. She had long brown hair with silver streaks, and her eyes were as green as the forest. She had pale skin and was around medium height.

"I'm here to help," Kendall said, sprinkling pixie dust on him. "I can't fix this, but I can get him back to the ocean faster. He'll be able to breathe temporarily, at least until we arrive. Take this crystal. It will show you when he gets home safe. Now, help me get him upstairs," she said, handing the crystal to Harper.

Once they had reached Harper's room, Kendall grabbed Bryce's hand and jumped out the window, flying toward the beach as fast as her wings could carry them.

"I'll be back," she shouted back at Harper.

As Kendall flew, she sprinkled more dust behind her and cast a spell to help Bryce remain calm.

"How are you doing?" she shouted.

"I'm okay," Bryce shouted back.

"We're almost there," she said.

Once they reached the ocean, Kendall set Bryce down on the sand, rolled him back into the ocean, and waited. Bryce swam up to the shore after a few minutes and thanked Kendall.

"You must be careful with the magic of the shell. We shall meet again," Kendall replied.

Then she flew back to Harper's palace and flew back inside the window she had jumped out of.

"Were you able to see on the crystal?" Kendall asked.

"Yes, thank you. I don't know what I would have done without you," Harper replied. "I know you're a pirate, but I must know, how did you fly earlier, and what was that dust you sprinkled on Bryce?"

"Can you keep a secret?" Kendall asked.

"Yes, you can trust me," Harper said.

Kendall then told Harper she was a pirate fairy and said, "I'm in charge of pixie dust that allows the Black Mist, our ship, to fly. I'm from an island called Encantra, where all creatures are unique and different from your world."

Harper intently listened to Kendall speak.

"I was born in a cave within a black mountain made of rocks. Inside that cave, there is a purple dust called pixie dust, or magic dust, as others have called it in the past. I am not sure how it got there; it was there even before my existence. I take care of it and use it to help others. Now that you know, let me introduce you to my crew of pirates. We are good pirates, and we help others in need. We are protectors, and our home base is on my island. The island is hidden and is not easy to find. It is guarded by magic. Come and join me downstairs when you are ready."

Kendall went downstairs and headed back into the ballroom. When she joined the others, the ball was in full swing. Dancing and laughter filled the cool, crisp air as it came in through an open window in the dining hall.

Harper came downstairs after changing into a more comfortable outfit, then went to meet with Kendall and the pirates. After the meet and greets, Captain Dawson told Harper that they were at Port Tilbury primarily to restock on supplies for the ship, including food and water, but that they were also in search of a ring that contained cursed powers. The captain also explained that they had seen a stranger lurking around Python Cove and the beach during their visits to Port Tilbury to restock. The description he gave Harper fit Raven Claw, and Harper began to think that Corbin was both her cousin and the stranger she had met at the marketplace. It would explain why he was always disappearing.

"The ring contains a charm so strong that if it falls into the wrong hands, it could be very fatal for us all. That is enough for tonight, though. We better head back to the ship, Captain Dawson said.

"Will you help us, Harper?" Kendall asked.

"Yes! But only if Bryce can come, too," Harper replied.

"Very well," Kendall said.

Harper then watched the pirates leave, waving goodbye. Later, she went upstairs for the night. With the window open, cold, crisp air crept into the room as she slept soundly.

***

The next day, Harper woke up to the sound of rain falling, so she decided to skip her visit with Bryce and use the time she had to create a list of things she might need to take with her the next day, when she was going to go and find the X she had uncovered at the beach.

As she wrote, Corbin snuck onto the roof of her palace, hid near the window, and waited for the opportune moment to ask her a question.

"Harper, what are you drawing? Is it a map? Or perhaps a picture of a ring?" Corbin asked.

Harper looked up and responded, "It is none of your concern. Now buzz off before I tell my father you're invading my privacy."

Corbin frowned and whispered, "I'll be back."

***

When the sun rose the next day, Harper grabbed her things and headed out to the beach to see Bryce. She jumped into the water and had Bryce sprinkle dust from the magic seashell on top of her so she could turn into a mermaid temporarily. She was planning to explore the reefs before digging up the X. However, not long after she started swimming through the Atlantic Ocean, she saw a killer whale.

"Bryce, look! It's an orca! They are one of my favorite animals. They're so beautiful," Harper said.

"Would you like to ride one?" Bryce replied.

"Yes, I would love to," Harper said.

Bryce then swam closer to the killer whale and pet its forehead. He grabbed Harper and placed her arms on the whale's top fin.

"Hold on tight," he said.

The whale swam with Harper on its fin for a good thirty minutes, and then she jumped off. Just then, a purple stingray swam through the water. Harper smiled and continued to explore.

Little did she know, Corbin had used a spell to transform into the stingray so he could keep an eye on her. He planned to trick her and see if she would reveal the location of the X she had found on her previous visit.

As Harper swam back to shore, Bryce used the magic seashell to turn human, despite his last incident. This time, he grabbed the dust and rubbed it on his legs like lotion, hoping it would change the way the magic worked.

"Okay, now we find this X," Bryce said.

"Look in the wet sand. The X is darker than the rest of the sand, almost like a black dust. We have to dig it up before the waves come back and hide it," Harper said.

Harper and Bryce both started to dig in the black-colored sand. They were both digging fast because the waves were coming back. The water crashed onto the sand shortly after they had started digging, making it harder for them.

"Keep digging fast. We will get to the bottom sooner," Harper said to Bryce.

"Okay, I will!" Bryce replied.

Halfway through digging in the sand, Harper and Bryce found a giant rock, and they were determined to dig it up. When they put their hands on the rock, it split into two and sent a sound wave across the beach, almost as if a spell had been broken.

"Hold on to my hands!" Harper said.

They held hands as the sand started to sink down on its own, moving in a swirling motion. They watched as the split parts of the rock fell into the swirling sand, disappearing beneath their feet. When the swirling sand had stopped, they let go of each other's hands. The water from the waves rushed into the hole they had dug up. They both walked over to the center of the hole and found a large black key strapped to the top of a black chest. Harper grabbed the key and opened the chest. Inside the chest was a large piece of felted fabric made of cotton. Harper picked up the fabric and gave it to Bryce, saying, "Unfold it. I am going to keep looking in the chest."

"Okay. Wait, Harper, look!" Bryce said.

Harper turned around to look at Bryce and saw him pointing to an opening that had formed next to where he was standing. It was shaped like a door.

"It has to lead somewhere! This fabric is a map, and it shows where that door opening leads," Bryce said.

"Let's explore it! But first, let's finish looking at all of this treasure. Look at all of these jewels. They are so beautiful," Harper said.

"Okay, but don't take too long. Who knows how long we have left to explore this underground cave," Bryce replied.

They both reached into the chest and began to dig through the jewelry and jewels in front of them. As they were looking, Harper picked up a necklace. It was a gold chain with a round crystal ball. Inside that ball were traces of black and purple sand. In the middle, there was an orca jumping into light-blue sand that seemed to represent the ocean's waves.

"I'm keeping this one," Harper said, looking at Bryce.

"Okay, you keep that, but you're going to want to see what I found," he replied. He opened his hands and showed Harper a small ring that was attached to a black chain. The ring had a purple sapphire in the middle, and it was surrounded by sparkling black diamonds. "I really like this one. I think I'll keep it."

"Wait! Bryce, I think that's the ring Captain Dawson told me about," Harper said.

"What?" Bryce said.

"You weren't there. Don't wear it. I'll explain later," Harper said.

"Okay, but I am taking it with me," Bryce said.

"Okay, let's go explore the cave. I'll close the chest and hold on to the key in case we need to come back," she said.

They then looked at the fabric they had found. The fabric had a map on it that had been painted with green and red paint. It showed footsteps leading the way to each destination. There were four items on the map, and they were shown in green. There was a book, a black chest, a seashell, and a key. The first one was the silver key.

"Let's go in order," Harper said.

They both walked through the door, only to find two different paths. One led to the right, and one led to the left.

"Which way do we go?" Harper said.

"Go left! The map states that the exit is on the right. Can we talk about what you meant regarding the ring now?" Bryce asked.

"Okay, the night you were flown back to the ocean by Kendall, Captain Dawson told me about a ring that was rumored to have strong magical powers. He didn't have any details about the color of the ring, but I have a feeling this could be it. He thinks that Corbin is after the ring, too. The pirates have been searching for it so that it doesn't fall into the wrong hands. We will have to tell them what happened when we get back to shore," Harper said.

"Oh no, that means Corbin will be after us. We need to be more careful about where we are keeping these treasures and when we bring them into the light," Bryce said.

"Okay," Harper replied.

Harper had told Bryce about her cousin on previous adventures, around when she'd first met him. She had also told him about the man named Raven Claw, whom she had met at the tavern the night she was in the marketplace.

Harper and Bryce both followed the blue-colored footsteps on the left until they reached an altar. Resting on it was a small navy-colored book. The book had a circle in the middle, and it looked like a jewel had fallen out of it. Harper picked up the book and read the first three lines of the writing inside.

"Bryce! It's a spell book!" Harper said.

"Wait, if this is a spell book, shouldn't you be careful? What if there are wicked spells inside?" Bryce asked.

"Good point. We will have to look through it thoroughly to see if there are any," Harper said.

As they were leaving, Harper noticed a blue backpack sitting on top of the altar. It had been underneath the spell book. As she got closer, the backpack opened its eyes and mouth and began speaking. Harper jumped, frightened by what she was seeing.

"Bryce, are you seeing this?" she said.

"Yes, I am. Do you think it's safe? And what are you going to name him?" Bryce replied.

"I think it's for the spell book, but we can put the rest of the items we find inside of it, too. I think I am going to name him Guzzle," Harper said.

"Okay, that sounds good. I was beginning to wonder how we were going to keep all of these items safe. Does he bite? I really hope not," Bryce responded.

"I don't think he'll bite us, but he might bite people if they try to take the items. I guess we will find out," Harper said.

Harper placed the spell book and the jewelry inside Guzzle and then continued to walk with Bryce. They saw purple footprints beginning to appear. They followed the footprints until they got to a rock that had the middle cut out of it. Inside the middle, they found a small black chest.

"Open it, Bryce!" Harper said

"It's locked, and there is no key. Let's take it and let Guzzle hold on to it until we can find a key to open it," Bryce said.

"Okay, let's look for the key before we continue," Harper said.

Harper and Bryce looked for a key underneath the rock; inside the middle, where the chest had been; behind the rock; and on top of the rock, but they could not find anything.

"Why would someone leave a chest with no key?" Harper said.

"I'm not sure, but I think we should move on to the next item. Who knows how long we have under here, and you know your dad isn't going to be happy if you've gone missing," Bryce said.

"Ugh! Okay, let's keep moving. Look, there are pink footprints now. Let's go!" Harper exclaimed.

Bryce and Harper kept walking and followed the pink footprints until they came to a circle in the ground. It was filled with water and seemed to be sitting on top of sand.

"Look on the ground. What is that? Is it safe to reach for the item?" Bryce said.

"I don't know, but there's only one way to find out," Harper said, sticking her hand into the water. She grabbed a medium-sized calico scallop seashell that looked like it had purple pixie dust inside. "I think this is more pixie magic, just like the other shell we found."

"Awesome! Let me see that. I'm going to sprinkle some of it on me so my fins don't come back just yet," Bryce said.

"Okay, look, there are the last set of footprints. This time, they are yellow. Let's go," Harper said.

Bryce followed her, and they continued their way around the cave until they reached a spot where there was a bright-yellow light shining through a carved hole in the cave's wall. Inside that hole was a gold key that had *Golden light does not open something bright. Find the chest and take the jewel that unlocks the spell* written on it. Harper grabbed the key after reading this, and the light that was shining went out.

"Bryce, this is it! It's the key that opens the chest," Harper said.

"How do you know? Let's try it first. I'll get the chest from Guzzle," Bryce responded, taking the backpack from Harper and knocking on Guzzle, who opened his eyes, looked at Bryce, and opened his mouth. Bryce reached inside and felt for the chest. Once he had located it, he pulled it out. "Okay, here. Try putting the key inside and see if it opens."

Harper took the key and opened the chest. She looked inside and saw an aquamarine jewel that was rather large. It had two clasps on the bottom.

"The spell book! Grab the spell book! This jewel belongs on top of it!" Harper exclaimed.

Bryce reached into Guzzle and grabbed the spell book, exchanging it for the key. He handed the spell book to Harper, and she placed the jewel on top of the rounded hole it had on it. The jewel clicked into place, and the words inside the book lit up in gold.

"What do you think this means?" Harper asked.

"I am guessing that if you read those spells now, something will actually happen, but I do not think right now is the best time to find out. Look! The walls are beginning to collapse. It's time to go! Put the spell book inside the black chest and close it. It will automatically lock. Then stick the chest inside of Guzzle. Hurry!" Bryce exclaimed.

Harper quickly did as Bryce said, and both of them ran toward the exit, following the right side of the cave until they came across the door that had led them inside. As soon as they walked through the door, the sand underneath them began to fill the hole and the door opening disappeared. The sand took them higher and higher, and then they were both back on shore, exactly where the X had been.

Harper looked around and saw that the sun was setting, then said, "Bryce, we have to go!"

"I know. I have no more time. My fins are back," Bryce replied.

"Okay, I'll meet you back here soon. My father will be wondering where I am. I am going to take Guzzle with me until we can figure out a safer place to put him," Harper said.

"Okay, be careful and make sure you tell Kendall about the ring," he replied.

The waves rolled in again, and Bryce swam off into the ocean. Harper watched until she could not see him any longer and then started her journey home. When she arrived at the palace, she headed straight to her room. Amber greeted her with kisses and hopped into her lap as she sat on her bed. Harper kissed her dog and wrapped her in a warm blanket.

"I'll be right back. I'm going to take a shower, and I'll be in bed next to you in no time," she said.

Amber stared at her, her tail wagging as if to say, "Okay, Mom."

After Harper had gotten cleaned up and changed, she placed Guzzle in her closet and shut the door. She then cuddled her dog until they were both sound asleep on her bed.

***

When Harper woke up the next day, she found a note that stated that her presence was required in the dining hall for afternoon tea. It was still early, so she decided to get ready for the day. Her hair was in long, bouncy curls, and she wore a feather-trimmed baby-blue headband. She wore a baby-blue mini dress that matched her hair accessory. It had lavender-colored lilies all over it. The dress also had baby-blue feathers sown onto the top part and the bottom of the sleeves, and her sleeves were very puffy and long. Her shoes were black flats, and they had a Velcro strap across to hold them down. They also had blue and lavender lilies all over them. Her makeup consisted of black eyeliner; a soft, blue-and-purple shadow; and black mascara.

When Harper was ready, she went down the stairs and walked into the dining room. As she looked around, she saw two tables. One was filled with three different types of tea sandwiches. One of the sandwiches had deviled egg yolks, egg whites, and lettuce. The second one had whipped cucumber, basil, plain Greek yogurt, cucumbers, and smeared butter. The last one had hummus, cranberries, and carrots. The same table had three different kinds of scones, including blueberry, cranberry orange, and lemon poppyseed. All three of these scones were gluten-free, sugar-free, and vegan friendly (Harper's favorite). The same table had three different kinds of chocolate-covered strawberries—white chocolate, dark chocolate, and a white-chocolate-and-lavender flavor. The next table had two tea pots, different colored teacups, and different kinds of tea, and there were sugar cubes, honey, lemon slices, and boiling hot water on a cart next to the table.

"Teatime is always my favorite," Harper said to her mother as she walked into the room.

"Good, because we have some special guests joining us today," Queen Skylar responded.

"Yes, we do. Take a seat on any of the couches, my dear," King Henry said.

Harper chose a seat next to the table with the tea. She watched as her aunt and cousin came into the castle and sat down on the couches across from her.

"I'm so glad you've come to visit, Arwen," Harper's mother said.

"Of course. It had been way too long," Arwen said.

"Kelsey, dear, why don't you go and sit next to Harper," Kelsey's father said.

As their parents socialized, Kelsey walked over to Harper's couch, and the cousins embraced each other.

"I'm glad you could all join us today," Harper said.

"Likewise," Kelsey replied.

Kelsey was wearing a medium-length baby-blue dress, with ruffles going down the bottom half of the dress. The sleeves were long and had ruffles that matched the bottom half. She was wearing a black gemstone necklace and a matching headband, and they both complimented her dress. Her long dark-brown hair was up in a smooth bun, a beaded hairband holding it together. She had also worn black flats to match. Each shoe had a strap that wrapped across it.

"Mother, may we please have some tea now?" Harper asked.

"Yes, darlings, dig in to both the tea and the food," Harper's mom replied.

Harper and Kelsey both reached for a teacup, and then the doorbell rang.

"Are we expecting more guests, dear?" Harper's mom asked.

"Yes, I invited a friend of mine and his wife to join us. I hope that's okay with everyone," King Henry said. He turned to the new guests and said, "Welcome, friends. Please help yourselves to some tea in the living room."

"Do you know who they are?" Kelsey whispered to Harper.

"No clue," Harper replied.

The girls helped themselves to some tea. Kelsey chose a white-peach tea and added a lemon slice and sugar cubes, and Harper chose a blueberry-and-lavender tea and added a lemon slice and honey.

While the girls drank their tea, King Henry introduced his wife and his relatives to his two new friends, saying, "This is King Niall Woods and his wife, Queen Jade. They are visiting from Sweden."

"It's a pleasure to have you joining us this morning," Queen Skylar said.

"Thank you. It's so nice to be here," Queen Jade said.

"Do you have any children?" Arwen asked.

"We do. We have a son. He loves to travel and go on his own adventures. That's where he is now, exploring the world," King Niall replied.

"An adventurer, huh? That sounds like fun. Maybe he can join us the next time we get together for tea," Tanner, Kelsey's father, said.

"Of course. We will be sure to invite him along next time," Queen Jade said.

"Let's try the food now," Kelsey said to Harper.

Kelsey began to try food with Harper, and they ate until they were full.

"May I have your attention, please? I am throwing a ball tonight, and it is requested that you all attend. Arwen and Tanner, let me show you to your rooms. King Niall and Queen Jade, you're welcome to stay in the guest bedroom downstairs. Skylar will show you to your rooms," King Henry said.

"A ball? Let's go get ready," Harper said to Kelsey, and they headed upstairs to Harper's room.

As everyone prepared for that evening, Harper and Kelsey spent time in Harper's room trying to pick out dresses and shoes for the night.

"What colors should we wear? I have stuff you can borrow in my closet," Harper said to Kelsey.

"I was thinking purple or lavender," Kelsey replied.

"Okay, I was thinking blue," Harper said.

The girls continued to look through Harper's closet until they found dresses to wear. Harper's dress was an aqua-blue ballgown with a sequined black belt at the waist. It had a strapless top, and peacock feathers covered the straps. Kelsey's dress was a lavender ballgown with long sleeves that were off the shoulder, and purple peacock feathers covered the top. The girls both chose black Mary Jane flats that matched their dresses. Harper's had aqua rhinestones, and Kelsey's had purple rhinestones. The girls continued to get ready and started curling and straightening their hair.

Around 4:00, King Henry's guests began to arrive. As Harper and Kelsey came down the stairs, dressed in the gowns they had chosen, Harper saw Bryce walk in, and she walked over to greet him.

"I'm so happy you're here," Harper said, hugging him. "How did you find out I was having a ball?"

"Kellan's parents called him and told him. His crew will be here later. And Kendall invited me. She figured it could be a fun night. We can all mingle," Bryce said. "Who's your lovely friend?"

"Oh yes, this is Kelsey, my cousin," Harper said.

"It is a pleasure to meet you, Kelsey, I'm Bryce, Harper's best friend, but you probably already knew that. Would you like to join me and get a bite to eat in the dining hall?" Bryce asked.

"Yes, I'd be delighted," Kelsey said.

The two then walked over to the dining hall for food. The tables had a wide variety of finger foods, tea, bubbly waters, and water, along with a self-serve salad station. The main meal was normally brought out after all of the guests had arrived and was usually set up next to the salad station.

Before Harper could join them, Kellan approached her and said, "Hey, Harper, I just wanted to say you look lovely this evening."

"Thank you. You look pretty great, too. Is the rest of the crew coming tonight?" Harper said.

"Yeah, they should be here later this evening. Care to join me in the dining hall?" Kellan said.

"I'd love to," Harper replied.

The two walked over to the dining room and each took a plate full of finger foods to the table where Bryce and Kelsey were sitting.

"There you are. I was wondering where you went," Kelsey said, smiling.

Just then, music came on, and King Henry's guests began to dance in the ballroom, which was across from the dining area. The music could be heard all throughout the castle. Harper got up to grab some tea from the dining table, and as she came back she saw Kendall and the pirates walking in.

"Kellan, Kendall's here with the crew," Harper said when she got back to their table.

"Okay, cool. Let them find us," Kellan replied.

After a few minutes of exploring the castle, Kendall spotted Kellan and walked over to where he was sitting with the rest of their crew.

"May we join you?" Kendall asked.

"Yes, we have some news we have been wanting to discuss with you," Bryce said.

Kendall and the pirates sat down and began eating some of the food they had grabbed in the dining area before heading over to the table.

Before Harper could say anything to the pirates, Kelsey excused herself, saying, "It's been a pleasure. Bryce, I hope you will write me soon, and I hope to see you again in the near future."

Kelsey tucked her chair in and walked toward her parents so she could meet and greet other guests who had arrived.

"Kelsey, why don't you come over for a piano lesson," Kelsey's mother said.

"Coming, Mother," Kelsey replied.

Once she had left their company, Harper looked at Bryce, and they both knew it was time to talk to the pirates about their last adventure.

"I'm glad you came tonight. Bryce and I discovered something the last time we were out at the beach. We were looking for an X on the beach and came across an entire new underground world. Among the items we found and brought back with us is a ring," Harper said.

"A ring?" Kellan replied.

"Yes, it is sterling silver and has a round purple sapphire on it," Bryce said.

"Do you have this ring with you?" Kendall asked.

"Yes, it's upstairs in a safe," Harper replied.

"We can show you if you'd like," Bryce said.

"Very well. Kellan, you better come along," Kendall said.

"The rest of you, wait here and watch for Corbin. I have a feeling he's going to make an appearance tonight, and the last thing we need is him spying on us," Harper said.

"Very well, Princess. We'll keep a weather eye out, but first let's grab a refill on these drinks," Captain Dawson said.

Harper smiled as she walked toward the stairs with Bryce, Kendall, and Kellan. When they reached the top of the stairs, they walked into Harper's room and shut the door behind them. Inside Harper's closet was a rug that covered a small door. It led to a secret passage, which was where Harper had placed the safe. Inside the safe were all of the treasures Harper and Bryce had found on the beach the last time they had visited, along with Guzzle. Harper grabbed the key for the safe from her jewelry box and opened the safe. Once opened, she grabbed the ring, came out, and shut the closet door behind her. Kellan, Kendall, and Bryce were waiting for her on the couch.

"Here it is," Harper said.

"Wow, I can see why you kept it," Kellan said, laughing.

"That ring is not an ordinary ring, Harper. Be careful with it. If it falls into the wrong hands, there's no telling what could happen," Kendall said.

"Aside from how beautiful it is, why is it so special?" Harper asked.

"This ring can reverse time to fix past events," Kendall said.

"However, it's a twin, and there is another just like it, but the other contains bad magic. This ring can cancel, overthrow, or outdo the other one with the correct spells. Despite this, it cannot reverse the damage its twin may cause; it can just reroute it or change certain things," Kellan said.

"If that's true, where is the twin? I only discovered one ring," Harper said.

"That is the mystery. We have tried, with Captain Dawson, to find the ring on numerous occasions but have failed,"" Kellan said.

"I think you should let Kendall take it for now," Bryce said.

"But what if we need it?" Harper asked.

"You could need it. For now, hold on to it. When you're done with it, you can give it to Kellan. He'll be in charge of it," Kendall said, and then she suddenly panicked. "Put it away! My pendant is glowing. Something isn't right. Kellan, go downstairs and see what's happening with Captain Dawson!"

As Kellan headed down, Bryce and Harper went down and put the ring back into the safe, locked it, and hid the key again. Kendall, Bryce, and Harper headed down into the dining room to catch up with the rest of the crew. By then, Harper had managed to change her shoes and tie her hair up into a bun.

"Captain Dawson, what's the latest news?" Kendall said.

"I saw Corbin. He was headed toward your bedroom a few minutes ago. Did you see him on your way out?" Captain Dawson said.

"The ring!" Bryce said.

"Wait, no! You must not leave the area, or he will know we are onto him," Kellan said.

"We will look for him. It is time to go now, boys. We'll catch up later, Harper," Kendall said, walking out with the crew, except for Kellan, who had stayed behind to talk to Harper. "Kellan, are you coming?"

"Yeah, give me a minute. I'll be out soon," Kellan said. "I hope I get the pleasure of having your company again soon, Princess," Kellan said.

"You will," Harper replied, smiling and waving as he left.

"It's getting late. Better help your parents start cleaning up," Bryce said.

"Okay, will you spend the night?" Harper asked.

"Sure, just tonight," Bryce replied.

After they had finished helping Harper's parents clean up, and after most of the guests had gone home, Harper and Bryce went upstairs to her room.

"How did the pirates know about Corbin?" Bryce asked.

"I told Kendall about him and the stranger I met at the marketplace the other night. She probably told the rest of the crew," Harper replied.

"I see. Well, I'm going to bed now. I'm tired. I'll see you in the morning," Bryce said as he walked into Harper's guest room, which was an extension of her bedroom.

After Bryce had gone to bed, Harper changed into more comfortable clothes and was about to go to bed when she heard a tap at her window. When she looked over at it, she did not see anything, so she walked back toward her bed, but then she heard another couple of taps. She walked over to her window, opened it, and said, "Hello? Is anyone there?" as she looked outside.

"Did I disrupt your sleep, Princess?" Kellan asked as he swung on a rope in front of her window.

"You scared me! What are you still doing here?" Harper replied.

"I had to tell you that the crew believes me about Corbin being up to no good," Kellan said.

"You were the one who told the crew about him?" Harper said.

"I had to. He's been sneaking around the marketplace, and I know he's your father's advisor, but I don't think he has King Henry's best interests at heart. After Kendall told me about the stranger you encountered the other night, I've been wondering if he's the same person. I mean, I have seen him in the marketplace, but never at the same time as Corbin. I'd watch him closely," Kellan said.

"He's being watched by the guards in the place, as well. We may be related, but I've never been close with him. Something about him rubs me the wrong way. Anyhow, enough about Corbin. Why did you leave?" Harper said.

"What do you mean?" Kellan replied.

"I heard your parents today. I didn't know they were your parents until they mentioned that they had a son during afternoon tea. Why did you run away? Or why did you decide to join the pirates crew you're in now?" Harper said.

"At the time, they wanted me to rule, and I wasn't interested in ruling a country, much less marrying a maiden of their choice. So, I packed my bags and joined Captain Dawson's crew one night as I was exploring the beach. I never looked back, and I can honestly say that I am happy with my decision. I do miss them often, but I always get opportunities to visit," Kellan said.

"I see. Well, I am glad you were able to see them tonight, though I don't think they recognized you," Harper said, smiling.

"Ever dream of setting sail on a flying pirate ship?" Kellan asked Harper.

"What? How does your pirate ship fly?" Harper replied.

"Now's your chance to find out," Kellan said, pointing toward the window. "The Black Mist awaits."

"I have to change clothes, and Bryce is in the other room. Can he come, too?" Harper said.

"We all have to change clothes, too. Better pack your things from the safe, change, and get Bryce ready, too. It's going to be a long night," Kellan said, grinning.

Harper went back to her closet to change, and she grabbed a backpack full of things she thought she would need. She left a note for her parents and then woke Bryce, saying, "Let's go.

Hurry and change. Get ready. We're going midnight sailing with Kellan and the crew."

"Ugh, okay. I'll grab my stuff. I'm sleeping on the ship, though," Bryce said.

After grabbing all of their stuff, the two friends got onto the windowsill. Kellan was waiting for them on the Black Mist, which Captain Dawson had parked next to the window.

"I'll set up the plank," Captain Dawson said.

"What? Are we diving into the sky?" Bryce asked.

"No, I'll sprinkle some pixie dust on you. That will make it easier for me to lift you onto the plank," Kendall said.

"You have wings!" Bryce said to Kendall.

"Yes, she's a fairy. Try to keep up," Harper replied.

"Okay, spread your arms out. I'm going to lift you," Kendall said.

"Okay," Bryce and Harper replied.

Kendall picked both of them up and placed them on the plank so that they could walk from the window to the pirate ship.

***

Once they were both aboard the Black Mist, Austin helped Bryce to the crew's quarters so he could get some rest. Kellan walked with Harper to the officer's quarters, which were next to the captain's cabin, and placed her stuff in an empty room that had a bed inside.

"You'll be comfortable here," Kellan said.

"Thank you," Harper said.

After she had set her things down and lain on the bed for a few minutes, Harper walked with Kellan to the forecastle deck.

As the ship sailed along under the starry blue-black sky, she could feel the wind against her face.

"I've always wanted this type of adventure. Thank you for inviting us along tonight," Harper said.

"You're welcome," Kellan said.

Kellan stared into Harper's brown eyes and gave her a look that every girl wants from a guy. Harper could not help but stare back into his bright-blue eyes, but before Kellan could make any moves, Barton interrupted, exclaiming, "Look on the dock. It's Raven Claw."

Kellan pulled out his spyglass, looked through it, and said, "That's him. I can't make out what he's doing on the dock, though."

Austin took out his binoculars and said, "Sprinkle that pixie dust, Kendall"

Austin dove off the same plank Bryce and Harper had used to get onto the ship. He flew through clouds and stopped on the third cloud down. He lifted his binoculars to his face and saw Corbin purchasing potions. He then flew back up to the Black Mist and said, "He's purchasing potions."

"I bet he's up to something, like brewing potions in his cauldron," Kellan said.

"We can't know for sure, but you may be onto something, Kellan," Captain Dawson said.

"Don't tell me we are going to let him get away without spying on him," Barton said.

"Tonight, we need to find resources. Let him go," Captain Dawson said.

"He's right," Kendall said.

As the pirates sailed on through the night, Harper got to know Kellan, and Kellan enjoyed her company as they discussed several topics of interest.

***

Meanwhile, back near the marketplace, Corbin experimented with the potions he had purchased, casting spells in his dungeon. He was determined to find the location of the other ring, and he wanted to know how to harm the killer whale Harper had encountered the last time she was on the beach.

"Why isn't this spell working?" Corbin said to his pet snake, Cosmo.

Cosmo was a ball python that had bright-blue skin. A pattern of black circles covered his body. He also had hints of forest-green inside the black lining on his body, and sometimes, from a distance, it looked like green glitter in the sun.

Corbin had found his companion along the same sandy beach that Harper had found the X on. He thought the sand had swallowed Cosmo. Instead, it had unintentionally scared the snake out of the tree he had been resting in. Cosmo had slithered away from the two trees he was near before the waves could sweep him into the ocean. Corbin had been looking for Harper, who was digging in the sand, when he found Cosmo, and he soon became attached to his new friend.

Corbin took good care of Cosmo and took him on most of his adventures, like the day he had spent at the marketplace. Corbin saw Cosmo as his travel buddy and someone he could talk to, though Cosmo seldomly replied.

While Corbin experimented with his potions, Cosmo, who had climbed onto a brick ledge in the dungeon, stared into the cauldron and hissed when it bubbled or boiled.

Chapter Two

Isla Mordaz

Back on the Black Mist, Bryce had woken up in the crew's quarters, and he was hungry. As he looked around for the crew, he spotted Mr. Nomad and walked over to where he was.

"I know it's late, but when are we eating? I can't remember having dinner last night. What time is it?" Bryce said.

"It's morning, but around here we have our lunch for breakfast, and we skip dinner because we have a late lunch and then a snack. Now, go wash up and get ready for the day," Mr. Nomad replied.

Bryce went to prepare for the day.

"Did we stay up and talk all night?" Harper asked Kellan.

"I'm afraid so. Better go get ready for another day. Breakfast is at seven."

"What are we having?" Harper asked.

"Minestrone and butter on toast. You can have some tea, water, or ginger beer with your meal, as well. The choice is yours," Mr. Nomad replied.

"I love minestrone, but isn't that a lunch dish?" Harper said.

"Depends on your perspective," Kellan replied.

"Agreed!" Kendall said.

Harper smiled and went to get ready for the day.

An hour later, Mr. Nomad rang a bell and said, "Food is ready," so Harper, Bryce, and the rest of the crew all headed into the captain's cabin, where Mr. Nomad, Bruce, and Barton had placed a blue tablecloth on a large table, along with soup, toast, butter, cheese, and a selection of drinks.

"Help yourselves," Mr. Nomad said.

"Will we be stopping at the garden this morning since Captain Dawson has already eaten?" Kellan asked.

"We are headed there now, and we will only stop for an hour," Mr. Nomad replied.

"What is the garden?" Harper asked.

"Oh, its lovely. We stop there on occasion to pick new flowers for the ship. They work as natural air fresheners," Kendall said.

After the pirates had finished their meals, Mr. Nomad, Bruce, and Barton cleaned up the area, and Harper, Kellan, and Bryce headed to the deck to see if they could spot the garden.

"Almost there," Kellan said.

As they flew over a lake, Harper spotted a quiet area that was uninhabited. It was full of grass and willow trees. In the middle of that field, there was a meadow full of all kinds of flowers.

"Oh, how beautiful!" Harper said, climbing down the ladder and going out into the field.

"Wait, Princess! You need your mask," Kellan yelled down to her.

"Mask?" she asked, confused.

"Yes, for the bees. You didn't think there would be any, did you?" Kellan said.

"Oh, I didn't think about it," Harper replied.

"Bryce has yours. He is coming down," Kellan said.

Bryce climbed down the ladder and handed Harper her mask. Kendall, Kellan, and Austin followed closely behind him. When Kellan had climbed down the ladder, Harper grabbed his hand and said, "Let's go," running toward the field.

The chemistry Kellan felt with Harper had always been there, but when Harper had grabbed his hand, the reaction between them left Kellan wanting more, though he wasn't sure what he wanted more of or why.

When they reached the field, Harper began to look for lilies. The lily was her favorite flower, and she preferred them in lavender and blue. While Harper looked for them, Kellan walked over to a field of roses and picked four of them—one lavender, one white, one pink, and one orange. Bryce was focused on peonies, and he chose four bright-pink ones. Kendall and Austin each grabbed a handful of dahlias in purple, orange, coral, pink, hot pink, and peach.

"Are we ready? Time is almost up," Austin said.

Harper had just spotted the lilies, and she quickly grabbed four of them—two blue ones and two lavender ones.

Kellan walked over to where Harper was and said, "I picked this rose just for you," handing her the lavender-colored one.

"Aww, thank you," Harper said, smiling. She then grabbed his hand and said, "Let's go. Time has expired!" then ran with him back toward the Black Mist.

Once the crew was aboard the ship again, they arranged the flowers and put different arrangements around the ship. Kendall then sprinkled a dust on them that would keep them fresh for the next three months.

"So that's why they last so long? Do you mind putting some of that on my rose?" Harper said.

"It won't last forever, but sure," Kendall said.

Harper put the flower in a vase, along with some water, and she placed it near her bed in the captain's cabin. Then she sat on the bed and fell asleep. She had spent the whole night getting to know Kellan and was tired.

When Bryce went by her room to see what she was up to and saw her sleeping, he asked Kendall if the crew could drop them off at the palace, saying, "I think we both need to rest for the rest of this day."

"Not to worry. I'll place her in her bed when we get there. Did you want a ride back to the beach? It's on our way," Kendall said.

"Yes, thanks," Bryce replied.

"Bring the ship down. We'll get back in the sea and drop Bryce off," Kendall said to Captain Dawson.

"Will do. Shall we fly back to the palace after that? It'll be quicker," Captain Dawson said.

"That's a plan," said Bruce.

The captain lowered the ship shortly after, dropping Bryce off near shore.

"Was great having you, mate," Kellan said.

"Likewise. I hope we can do it again," Bryce replied.

After they had dropped Bryce off, the pirates sailed in the air, heading to Sterling Krystalline. When they got there, Kendall gently lifted her with pixie dust, and Kellan grabbed her flower. Kendall put Harper on her bed in her room, and Kellan placed her flower on the counter near her bed.

"I'm keeping the treasure for safekeeping. Corbin will find it if I don't," Kellan said to Kendall.

"Very well," Kendall replied.

When they left, Captain Dawson sailed the Black Mist in the ocean for two hours, traveling through heavy rain, heading to a hidden island so Kellan could hide the treasure for Harper. The location was not known to those who had never been to it. The island was hidden by giant rocks that blocked the view from passing sailors. Plus, the weather was normally gloomy in that part of the ocean. Once the Black Mist was near the cobalt rocks, it disappeared underneath the ocean waves. When the ship had come back up to the surface, it was near the shore of Isla Mordaz.

"Be quick," Captain Dawson said to Kellan.

Kellan climbed off the ship and began to hike to the center of the island, where there were four different paths to choose from. After he had thought about which path to take, he decided to head into the rainforest. He figured there were more hiding spots, and it was also the least enticing choice out of the four terrains. Once Kellan had found a spot to hide the items, he returned to the Black Mist, and the ship sailed back into the open ocean.

***

The next day, Harper awoke to a dark, cold, and gloomy morning. She could hear raindrops hitting her window. She loved the rain. She got ready for the day, and after breakfast she grabbed her bag and raincoat, along with her waterproof boots, and headed out to the beach to meet up with Bryce.

"Let's go see what other cool jewelry we can find in the treasure chest," Harper said.

"In this rain?" Bryce replied.

"Yes, come on!" Harper said.

So, both Harper and Bryce walked over to the X and began to dig it up quickly. Once they had dug halfway into the sand, the hole closed, just like it had the last time they were there, and the rain stopped.

"It looks exactly the same as the last time we were here," Bryce said.

"Let's go see what we can find," Harper said.

Harper and Bryce walked on the same path and headed right, searching for the treasure chest. Before they could get to it, Harper saw a green light coming from a dark cave.

"Bryce, look!" she said.

They both walked over to it, and Harper saw a large black pouch made of velvet. She took the pouch off the tall, rounded, fossilized, wooden plinth and found that the pouch was heavier than she had anticipated.

"Bryce, come here. Hold the pouch. It's heavy. I'm going to open it and see what's inside," Harper said.

"Okay, I've got the base. Let's see what we find," Bryce said.

Harper carefully opened it and reached inside, then said, "Wow, there are gems inside. I love the baby-blue ones. I'd love to take one, but let's see what else is in here." She took all of the gems out and placed them on the plinth. At the bottom of the pouch, she found a small, rolled-up scroll. She opened it and said, "It has a message. 'When the key is what you seek, find the serpent that is meek.' Serpent? But what serpent?"

Bryce started to look through the pile of gems, and something stood out.

"Harper! The gems! They have snakes on them. Look at the blue ones. If you look in the light, you can see them," Bryce exclaimed, putting the gems under the green light.

"But why only the blue ones?" Harper asked.

"I'm not sure, but I've checked all of them, and these are the only ones that carry that symbol," Bryce replied.

"Let's take the ones with the symbol. I have an inkling that we will need them later on. Let me make room for them in my bag," Harper said. When she opened her bag and looked inside, she was shocked to find that it was filled with small rocks. "Bryce! No! The treasure from last time is gone!"

"What? How?" Bryce asked

"Someone must have stolen it," Harper said.

She dumped the items out of the bag, and out came a paper with a note. *I took your treasure to keep it safe. -Kellan*

"Oh, thank goodness. Kellan has it. There's a note," Harper said, showing Bryce.

"Ugh, good grief. My heart skipped a beat. Let's put these gems in your bag already. I'm sure the treasure will be fine with Kellan watching after it," Bryce replied.

"Okay, load up my bag. You'll have to carry it," Harper said, laughing.

"Hey, why me? I see how it is," Bryce replied, laughing.

After they had loaded all of the gems inside her bag, they walked in the same direction as before, and it was not long until they reached the treasure chest.

"Let's open it. Do you still have the key?" Bryce said.

"Yes, it should be in the front pocket of the bag," Harper replied.

Bryce checked the pocket and found the key inside. He opened the chest and began to look at all of the treasure. Harper joined him, and after looking closely she saw a hidden latch at the bottom of the chest.

"This wasn't here before," Harper said, looking at Bryce.

"Did you notice the design of the chest? I didn't know it had a snake before, either," Bryce replied.

"That's because it wasn't there last time," Harper said.

"Look, there's another scroll. It says, 'Set a marked gem inside and trade for the green ring outside. Use the snake to bend into form, or never see the ring perform,'" Bryce said.

"It mentions a snake. A live one?" Harper replied.

"I think so, but where? I do not see any live snakes around here, or in or around this chest," Bryce said.

"Me either, but this does mention putting a gem in the latch. It's the first part of the puzzle. I'm going to reach into my bag and place one inside the chest," Harper said.

"Okay, choose a dark-blue one," Bryce replied.

Harper placed the dark-blue gem inside the chest after she opened the latch.

"We're going to have to come back to look for that snake another time," Harper said, rereading the words on the scroll.

"The ring must be a key, because the map mentioned a key, and if the map wasn't in your bag, Kellan must have it," Bryce said.

"Check the bag again. I have a hidden compartment inside," Harper said.

Bryce searched the bag again and found the map inside the hidden compartment. He opened the map to read and study it again.

"The ring does turn into a key. The photos and the writings make sense. I don't know what else it could be. The point is that this key should open a passage," Bryce said.

"A passage? To where?" Harper said.

"I'm not sure, but look, we found the other ring. It's an emerald-green color, and it's gorgeous," Bryce said, picking it up.

"Good looking out. I almost overlooked that. You can put it inside Guzzle for now. Let's look through the treasure again and see if we can find another clue," Harper replied.

Harper and Bryce looked through the treasure again looking closely as they searched for more clues.

"I found it!" Bryce exclaimed.

"How do you know?" Harper said.

"I know because it has the same symbol the gems have, and it's more of a blue-black color," Bryce replied, handing the bottom half of a key to Harper, who put it in her bag.

"We have to tell the pirates what we found," Harper said

"We will, but first let's get back to the castle. I'm starving," Bryce replied.

Harper and Bryce buried the chest before leaving, ensuring that no one would find it, and then they headed out of the hole, going in the same direction they came in. When they finally climbed out of the hole, they both refilled it with sand, and the waves crashed over the sand, smoothing it out and making it look like nothing had been there. They walked to Sterling Krystalline and when they arrived Harper was surprised to see Kellan sitting at the dining table.

"Kellan? What are you doing here?" Harper said.

"I thought I'd drop by and see how you had been doing since the other night. I see you have your bag," Kellan said.

"I'm good. I know you took the treasure and hid it. I found the key and the map," Harper said.

"We have a lot to tell you about our morning," Bryce said.

"I'd love to hear it," Kellan replied.

"Oh good, you're here. Your friend told us you were expecting him, so your mother and I set up a tea bar with tea, honey, lemon, ice, and hot water, along with a salad bar. There are also cucumber sandwiches and deviled eggs for lunch," King Henry said after he and Queen Skylar had walked up to them.

"Thank you, Daddy!" Harper said

"Thank you, sir. We appreciate it," Bryce said.

"Very well. Your father and I will be running some errands and will be back in the afternoon. Have fun," Queen Skylar said, and she and King Henry headed out to their carriage, waving.

Once the door had shut behind them, Harper and Kellan headed over to where the food was set up.

"Let's start with some tea. I am going to get some jasmine green tea, and I'll add honey and coconut milk and pour it over ice," Harper said.

"I think I'll take the same thing," Bryce replied.

"I'm going to do a honey-and-mango green tea over ice," Kellan said.

When the three friends had finished getting their drinks and food, they all sat down at the dining table, and they talked and ate. Bryce and Harper told Kellan about their adventure back at the ocean earlier that day.

"You have the ring? We have to tell Kendall," Kellan said

"Yes, you should. I trust you to keep this in a safe place. I'll let you hide it where you put the other treasures," Harper replied, giving the ring to Kellan, who put it inside a locket around his neck.

"Will you have dinner with me?" Kellan asked aloud.

"Tonight? Me or Harper?" Bryce asked.

"Both of you. I would like to show you where I've chosen to keep the treasures, just in case you need them in the future. Kendall will be there, too," Kellan said.

"Of course. If not tonight, when can we expect to join you?" Harper said.

"This weekend. I'll stop by your window. Make sure you leave a note for your parents, Harper. For now, I must go thank your parents for lunch. I will take another tea to go. I've got to get back to the crew. Pirates' life," Kellan said.

After Kellan left, Harper walked Bryce back to the ocean and asked, "Do you have the magic? I can stay for a few hours before I head back home. Let's go swimming!"

"Yes, ready?" Bryce said.

"Yes, ready!" Harper shouted.

Bryce sprinkled mermaid dust on Harper, and they both dove into the deep ocean.

"The water is great today. I hope we run into our killer whale friend. What shall we name him?" Harper said.

"I think I'm going to call him Dash-ren because he is really quick when he swims. He's the king of speed in the ocean. I think he could catch up to the Black Mist, or any other ship or sea creature, in a matter of seconds," Bryce said.

"I like that name. I hope he responds to it if we see him today," Harper replied.

Harper and Bryce swam deeper into the ocean, looking for coral reefs so they could collect rare seashells. Harper liked collecting them and then selling her collection at the marketplace. Sometimes, when she was feeling creative, she would make jewelry to sell, such as earrings, bracelets, and necklaces.

As Harper and Bryce were exploring, Harper saw a black fin and swam up to the surface.

"It's Dash-ren. I knew you would come back," she said, hugging him.

"There you are, boy. We missed you," Bryce said.

Bryce and Harper climbed on Dash-ren's back and let the orca take them for a ride.

"Woo-hoo! This feels amazing," Bryce yelled.

They spent the rest of the afternoon with Dash-ren, playing games with him, feeding him fish, and exploring the salty ocean. When the sun started to set, Harper knew it was time to go.

"Don't worry, Dash-ren. We will be back another day. Stay safe out here," Harper said as they both swam in the other direction, heading toward shore. "Let's go, Bryce. I have a feeling we will have guests tonight for dinner."

"Okay, race you back to shore," Bryce said, swimming away quickly.

When they reached the shore, he sprinkled the magic on Harper and watched her tail transform back into legs.

"I love having both," she said.

"Me, too! It's the best of both worlds," Bryce said.

"Are you coming with me tonight?" Harper asked.

"No, I am having dinner with some of my friends tonight," Bryce said.

"Very well," Harper replied, starting her walk back to the palace.

When Harper arrived back home, she was greeted by Amber.

"She's missed you," Harper's mother said.

"Take her out with you tomorrow," her father said.

"Okay, I can do that! Hi, girl, I missed you," Harper said to her dog, giving her kisses, and then she turned to her parents and said, "I'm going to take Amber on a stroll before dinner."

"Okay, don't be gone too long. Dinner will be here in thirty minutes," Harper's mom said.

"Okay," Harper replied.

***

Once Harper had walked her dog and brought her back inside, she gave her a rawhide-free bone and headed upstairs to clean up and change. Once she was ready, she came into the dining area.

"Kellan?" Harper said.

"Oh, you two know each other?" King Niall asked.

"I think you misheard me, sir. I said 'Hellen.' She was a local I met at the marketplace. At first glance, I thought Mrs. Woods looked like her. I do apologize," Harper replied, blushing

"Oh, that's quite all right, dear. This is our son, Kellan," Queen Jade said, pointing to Kellan. "He's here visiting us, and we thought you should meet him. After all, you're within his age group, and well, it doesn't hurt to have friends in high places." She winked.

"Hi, Kellan, I'm Princess Harper," Harper said, staring at him awkwardly.

"Well, you two can come over here and help yourselves. You must be starving. We're having seltzer water and pasta. There is a buffet across from the dining table, and some salad, as well. Please help yourselves. We'll be having tea later, as well," King Niall said.

"Thank you, Your Highness," Harper said, bowing.

Harper's and Kellan's parents walked back to their seats and continued to socialize, and Harper was left with Kellan at the dining table.

"Way to save us both with your marketplace lie," Kellan said, grinning.

"Sorry, I had no idea your parents would be joining us tonight," Harper said.

"It's all good. Want to explore the food with me?" Kellan replied.

"Yes, please. What kind of pasta do we have today?" Harper asked.

"Well, we have meat sauce and corkscrew pasta, fettuccini alfredo, cheese ravioli, and macaroni and cheese with smiley pasta," Kellan said.

"Smiley pasta? Ha!" Harper said, laughing.

"Yeah, well, they look like smiles or rainbows," Kellan replied.

"I can see that. I think I am going to try a small amount of all of them. The salad looks amazing, as always," Harper said.

"Yes, it does. You can never go wrong with it. It is my favorite because you can also top it with anything," Kellan replied.

They both served themselves and got their drinks of choice. The two friends spent the evening talking, their parents watching from a distance.

"I think our parents like that we're friends," Kellan said.

"Yeah, they've been eyeing us all night," Harper said.

"Can you get away tonight?" Kellan replied.

"I can try. What do you have in mind?"

"Well, I'm ready to show you and Bryce where I've hidden the treasure. The journey is long and will take a day or two," Kellan said.

"Okay, can we leave around four a.m. this time? I need some sleep," Harper replied.

"Okay, I'll pick Bryce up and then come and get you. I'll go tell my parents that I'm leaving and let Kendall know that we're going to go explore the island," Kellan said.

"Island? You hid the treasure on an island?" Harper replied.

"I know you're thinking it's going to be small. This island, however, is quite big. It's hidden from sight, covered by a set of rocks that surrounds it on the outside, so travelers are fooled into thinking it's a set of rocks resting on the ocean. Enough about it, though. I'll let you see it for yourself when we get there," Kellan said.

"Very well. I'll see you soon," Harper said, hugging Kellan.

Kellan walked over to his and Harper's parents and thanked them for the meal, then left the manor. Harper then dismissed herself, as well, and headed upstairs to pack and rest before her trip.

***

The next day, Harper awoke to the sound of her alarm and thought, *Oh no, I overslept.* She got ready for her day quickly, then took Amber with her on a hike. After three hours of walking with her dog in the sun, Harper returned to Sterling Krystalline; set Amber up with food, treats, and water; and went to go take a shower. After she had showered and gotten dressed for the day, she went downstairs for lunch.

"I took Amber on a three-hour hike," Harper said to her mother.

"Oh, okay. Well, at least she got some sun. She seems tired, so we'll let her rest for now, and you can go about your day," Harper's mother replied.

Harper went to the kitchen and was fixing herself a sandwich when she heard a knock on the window. She walked over to the window and saw Kellan.

"What happened?" Harper said.

"What do you mean? I guess I figured the time you gave me was too early, so I decided to drop in at one p.m. so that you could do what you needed to do. I figured we could also pack up some food for our journey. I've brought silver to pay for it all. That way, your parents can go and buy more food for themselves. We are short on time now," Kellan said, grinning.

"Ugh, okay, fine. Come inside. I'll go grab my backpack and bring a separate bag down for the food," Harper replied, then went upstairs. She came back down with a cooler that Kellan could put all of the food in and said, "Knock yourself out," handing it to him.

Kellan grinned, shaking his head, and filled the cooler with items from inside Harper's fridge, then said, "Okay, that's the last of it. I've left the silver on the counter. I wrote your name by it."

"Okay, let's go. I'm ready if you are," Harper said.

***

Once Harper was on the Black Mist, she went into her quarters to put her bag down. Kellan headed into the kitchen to give Mr. Nomad the food he had gathered, and Mr. Nomad began working on a dinner recipe. Back on the deck, Bryce was speaking to Austin, and Captain Dawson was steering the ship.

The Black Mist had gone from flying in the air to sailing in the ocean. The crew could feel the turbulence of the ship as it went across the waves of the sea. The ship was headed north for a while, which gave Harper a chance to interact with Kellan again. Bells rang on the deck as Mr. Nomad let the crew know dinner had been served.

"Head to the captain's quarters," Austin said aloud.

Once the crew was inside and dinner was served, everyone ate, and engaged in conversation, until there was no food left.

"The salad, baked ham, and potatoes were really good. I especially liked the dressing you chose," Bryce said.

"Me, too," Barton said.

"Thanks, lads," Mr. Nomad replied.

"The winds have changed. We're heading into rain. Prepare the deck, lads!" Captain Dawson said.

"Aye aye, Captain!" the crew replied.

The crew began to prepare for a possible thunderstorm. The skies turned black, and the rain began to sprinkle down onto the ocean's facet, and onto the Black Mist. The wind had grown cold and crisp, blowing against the crew's faces. The weather stayed this way all through the night. The rain fell softly, and the wind blew gently, even as Harper, Bryce, and the pirates slept below the ship's deck. The pirates sailed straight, going north until the next morning. When they had awakened from their slumber, Harper and Austin walked out onto the deck.

"It's still gloomy out, but I see some blue in the sky, and the rain has cleared," Austin said.

"Aw, I was hoping it would rain for a few days. I love it," Harper replied.

"It happens more often than not. You'll get your fix," Austin said.

Captain Dawson had been listening to them talk, as he had not left the steering wheel since the crew had boarded the ship. He normally took turns with Mr. Nomad, but since Mr. Nomad needed rest, he had decided not to switch.

"Princess, we're heading south now, going straight for a while. It shouldn't be long until we reach Isla Mordaz, in case you were wondering," Captain Dawson said.

"Isla Mordaz? So that is what it's called? Kellan failed to give me that detail. Why is it called Mordaz?" Harper asked walking over to where to he was.

"Mordaz is Latin for gaze. The legend says that travelers and other pirates could not stop gazing at the island because of the honed, cobalt rocks that surround it. The rocks are also what prevents most pirates from venturing onto the island. The outer appearance of this island has struck fear into sailors and pirates alike," Captain Dawson said.

"Mist also surrounds the outer rims, and it can be difficult to see," Kellan said.

"Well, at least we know the treasure is safe now," Bryce said.

"Yes, that is why we chose it," Kendall replied.

The pirates sailed on the cool ocean for half the day, then reached a location to the far left of them, where it was overcast.

"We're here," Kellan said to Harper, handing her a telescope. "Look through my pirate's spyglass."

Harper looked into the spyglass and could see tall, sharp rocks in the distance. They seemed to go on forever. The rocks were black, but they faded into a bold cobalt, almost like mineral rocks found in caves. They were beautiful yet subtle, so they did not reflect the sun (if there was ever any sun in the area. Considering the surrounding doom, it didn't seem like it). Harper could also see the mist that surrounded the island. She was thrilled about the weather and liked the dark aspect of it all, but she was curious if that would all change once she was on the island.

"Have you actually been on Isla Mordaz?" Harper asked Kellan, handing the telescope back to him.

"I have. Why do you ask?" Kellan replied.

"Is it different once you set foot on the island?" she asked.

"You'll have to see for yourself," Kellan said.

"How on earth do we get there?" Bryce said as they got closer.

"Drop the anchor, mates," Captain Dawson shouted.

"Aye aye, Captain," Bruce and Barton replied.

"It's time. Grab your bag, Harper, and prepare to go ashore with Kendall, Austin, and Bryce. The rest of the crew will keep watch for travelers and other pirates," Kellan said.

"Other pirates?" Bryce said

"Yes, there are other pirates out in these waters," Bruce replied.

"But how will you hide the ship? It's too obvious out here," Bryce replied.

"You'll have to trust the captain on that one, mate," Mr. Nomad said.

"Everyone, grab ahold of something. We're going under," Captain Dawson said.

Harper had walked over to the captain's quarters to grab the backpack she would need on the island, so she was nowhere in sight when Kellan looked around.

"Harper! Where are you?" Kellan said, running over to the captain's quarters.

"I'm over here, silly. Got my stuff. What are you yelling about?" Harper asked.

"We're going under," Kellan replied.

"What?" Harper said, surprised.

"Just grab on to me," Kellan said, pulling her closer to him.

Harper grabbed his shirt and hugged him tightly, and Kellan grabbed ahold of a post inside the room with both his arms and a hiking gun, making sure he had a secure grasp on it.

Captain Dawson cast a spell on the ship, saying, "The sea and wind stir. Create a blur and sink us down near the ground, down deep, and raise us up on shore for those who know to explore treasures galore."

Immediately after that, the Black Mist began to sink.

"Hold your breath. The water will come inside," Kellan said.

"Okay, I will," Harper said.

As the ship began to sink, Harper could see the fish and sea creatures swimming in the ocean, and she focused her gaze on them until she saw the island's bottom rock compilation. Her eyes grew big. The island was not only huge in size, but it also, from her perspective in the ocean, looked like a skeleton with hair. The eyes and nose of the skull looked like they had been punched out, and so did the bottom. The ship seemed to begin to go underneath it.

Harper closed her eyes, and before she could open them, she heard Kellan's voice saying, "Harper, open your eyes. You can breathe again. We're on the shore of the island."

"We are? Tell me what I saw in the ocean wasn't real," she said, staring up at him, her arms still around him.

"It was real. You weren't dreaming, Princess. You can let go now," Kellan said, grinning.

"Oh, right! I knew that," Harper said, letting go of his waist.

"Ready to explore?" Kellan asked.

"Yes, I am. I'm going to go find Bryce," Harper said.

Once Harper had found Bryce, she went up to the deck of the Black Mist, and when she looked out at the island in front of her, she was amazed by its beauty.

"It's beautiful, and so lush! It resembles the outside a bit, but I don't doubt that can change at any time," Harper said.

"I thought we would be near the island, though. It seemed like we were so close when we were underwater," Bryce said.

"Cheer up, mate. We're not too far off," Barton replied.

It was sprinkling as the crew drew closer to the island. Once the pirates had arrived, they left the Black Mist on the sandy black shores and walked toward the green inlands of the island.

"Is there volcanic activity on this island?" Harper asked Kendall.

"No, there isn't, but there are mountains that resemble volcanoes," Kendall replied.

"Oh, thank goodness!" Harper replied.

"So, where on this gigantic island did you hide the treasure? And are you sure others won't be able to come here?" Bryce asked Kellan.

"It's in the rainforest, inside the 20185581521195. I never said others wouldn't be able to come here. They very well can. I just said there were obstacles along the way, and on the island that would make it more difficult," Kellan replied.

"Shhh! Don't give away the location out loud. You don't know who is here and who's listening," Kendall said, scolding Kellan.

"Sorry, I won't be repeating that," Kellan said.

"What? You gave a number at the end. What is that supposed to mean?" Harper said.

"I'll explain when we get there. For now, let's focus on crossing this river that's coming up," Kellan said, pointing to an open plain.

"It's gorgeous. Oh, look, there's dinosaurs!" Harper exclaimed.

"Those are brachiosaurs. They are harmless. They can lead us to the destination, but first let's have some snacks by the water. I have apples and golden cheese crackers. Everyone can have a baggy and a water," Kendall said, passing them out.

"I'm going to explore the water before I eat," Harper said.

"All right, but be brief," Kendall replied.

As Harper dove into the water, Kellan handed Harper's bag to Bryce, saying, "Guard it while she swims."

As Harper was in the water, it became clear, and she could breathe without holding her breath. Before she knew it, she had turned into a swamp mermaid. These mermaids were different from ocean mermaids. They had jagged-edged fins on their feet and hands, and along their waists, and they looked like humans but meaner. As Harper continued to explore, she spotted Corbin. She stayed quiet as she observed him, hiding in the kelp.

As Corbin explored the lake, he discovered a secret passageway in the bottom layer of the lake, and it went underneath Isla Mordaz. He lifted the latch that was attached to a door, and he saw that the layers of water didn't mix. He was shocked and yet still curious. Before he could dive into the ocean water, he spotted a great white shark swimming in the space. It had a blue glow about it. He was curious about that and decided he would return to the lake instead of exploring the ocean more. Little did he know, a curse had been placed on the shark as well as any pirate or explorer who came across that portion of the island. But adventurers would need to get inside the water in order for the curse to be placed on them, and since Corbin had only looked at the shark, he was free for now. Looking around to make sure the coast was clear, Corbin closed the copper door, swam up to the surface, turned into a raven, and flew away.

When Harper saw he was gone, she swam up to the surface and said, "Did you see him? Please tell me you saw him!"

"See who?" Kellan asked

"Corbin. He's here. He found a copper door with a latch. It leads to the ocean and a shark! He hesitated to jump in, although he was going to, and then he transformed into a raven. He is Raven Claw! He has to be! That explains so much. Oh, and I also turned into a swamp mermaid," Harper exclaimed.

"Glad you're having fun exploring," Kellan said, grinning.

"Jokes aside, if Corbin is Raven Claw, he's up to something. We need to make sure he doesn't get ahold of the other ring before we do," Kendall said.

"I agree, but how do we even know where it is? I do not think it is on this island, but he could use the space and hide it here. Better get a move on before he claims the space we've hidden our treasure in," Austin said.

"He's right. Here is your food, Princess," Mr. Nomad said, handing Harper her food.

"Thank you, Mr. Nomad. I will eat it while we walk to our next location," Harper replied, smiling.

***

As the pirates walked toward the location in the rainforest, Corbin had found a spot to land. There was a small cave located near a small river that had luscious succulents, wildflowers, and plants surround it, and the cave was housing Cosmo. He had left Cosmo behind because he had been afraid the snake would not be able to swim in the lake. Corbin landed near this cave, turned back into his human form, and headed inside. He picked up his spell book and began reading the pages and looking for two spells.

"There has to be something in here about a snake breathing underwater, and something to put that shark to sleep," Corbin said aloud.

After an hour of searching the book, Corbin came across a spell and read aloud, *"'Freeze motion, stop time, pass the danger to explore the ocean floor, petrify, pause, discover.'"*

At the bottom of the page, the spell stated that it would work for only two hours, and an underwater timer was attached to the page.

"At last! This is it! It's the spell I need," Corbin said to his snake, grinning.

The spell came with directions and listed the items needed to make the potion. "One lavender twig, two handfuls of star-shaped leaves, two fish gills, two shark teeth, and one set of bat wings. Time to visit a witch's lair," Corbin said aloud, laughing an evil laugh.

He left Cosmo behind, leaving him with plenty of berries, nuts, and water.

"I'll be back soon, my pet," Corbin said.

Cosmo hissed as he slithered about in a circle.

Corbin turned himself back into a raven and flew toward the back end of the island, near a mountain that looked like a volcano. When he landed, he looked around for a small cottage that was located in the bottom portion of a tree. It was said to be the home of two witches who housed items used for potions and spells. The witches were named Belinda and Clementine, and they both lived in the portion of the island called Ebony Woodlands. No sunlight ever got inside the area, as black and navy-blue clouds hung in the skies above it, and rain always drizzled on that part of the island. More than one witch and wizard lived in Ebony Woodlands. All of their homes were made from the trees that were there, as they were exceptionally large and tall, but only one home looked like a cottage, and that was the home of Belinda and Clementine. The two friends had been living together since they had turned twenty-one, and they were now in their late twenties. Corbin sought to speak to them both and see if he could exchange his silver for items on the spell's list.

Once Corbin had turned back into human form, a wizard from the village approached him and asked, "Who do you seek?"

"I need to speak with Belinda and Clementine. I need to purchase a few items from their shop," Corbin replied.

"Follow me. Have you visited them before?" the wizard replied.

"No, but my parents used to speak of their parents. When I was young, we had a playdate, and I remember so clearly that it was here on Isla Mordaz. It is how I found the island. My parents kept a map, and when they passed away, they left their small home to me. I was able to find my way here. I just hope they remember me," Corbin said.

After walking for thirty minutes in Ebony Woodlands, Corbin could see the cottage of the two witches. Smoke was coming out of the chimney.

"We have arrived. Good luck to you, and if you should need anything, please do not hesitate to ask. I have a smaller cottage near the entrance of the dark forest, and it is my job to attend to guests. That is where you can find me if you should need anything," the wizard said.

"Thank you," Corbin replied, then walked up to the cottage's door.

The cottage was a soft gray color, and tree-star plants covered the outside. Lavender plants draped down the roof. Corbin knocked on the door and waited for a response.

When the witches heard there was someone at the door, they looked through the peephole in the door to see who it was before opening the door.

"It's a guy. He looks familiar," Clementine said.

"Hmm, I do not think we have met him before. He does not look like one of our regular customers, but he could also be a visitor of the island. Are we letting him in? It's almost time for tea," Belinda said.

"Yes, let him in. He looks cold enough, standing in the rain. Since he is visiting during non-visiting hours, I'm curious about what he wants. Or maybe he's just unaware since it's his first time here," Clementine said.

"Just open the door before he changes his mind," Belinda said.

Clementine opened the door, Belinda by her side, and they said, "How can we help you?"

"I do not know if you remember me. My name is Corbin. We had a playdate when we were younger. That's how I found your cottage. I got a map of the island from my parents. They have since passed away, but I need to purchase a few ingredients from you, if you have them. My mother left a note for me that said you possess magic," Corbin said.

"Come inside. What items are you looking for? I can show you what we have out back and inside," Belinda said, shutting the door.

"Oh, wait, are you hungry or thirsty? We were just about to have tea from our tea sampler. We have salad, cucumber sandwiches, and scones to go with it, and the sampler has, like, four different teas," Clementine said.

"I'd like that," Corbin said, smiling.

"Great! I'll get the items ready, and you can relax at the table," Belinda said.

"So, what items do you need? Maybe I can grab them for you while we wait on Belinda. I can still show you around afterward," Clementine said.

"I can show you my list," Corbin said, handing her the paper.

"We have all of that. It has actually been prepackaged as a random order. We have three left from earlier today," Clementine said.

"Tea is ready," Belinda interrupted.

"I'll grab your items after we eat," Clementine said to Corbin, twirling her hair.

"Help yourself, Corbin," Belinda said, pouring him a cup of tea.

"Oh my, I forgot to ask you. What kind of tea do you like? This one is lavender and basil, but we also have blueberry, lemon, Cardamone and honey, and mango green tea. Which do you fancy?" Belinda asked Corbin.

"I guess I'll try the lavender-and-basil tea since I can't decide. They're all great choices," Corbin said.

After he had taken a sip of the lavender, he put his teacup down and made a funny face.

"Let's trade, Corbin. Lavender-and-basil tea is my favorite. You can take the mango," Clementine said, grinning.

"How did you know I'd choose the mango?" Corbin asked.

"Although I didn't recognize you at first, I will admit to remembering the playdate, and I remember that your flavor of choice was always mango when our moms would make tea candies for us," Clementine said.

"You remember that?" Corbin asked.

"Yes, I do," Clementine said, smiling.

The two witches and Corbin spent the next hour and a half catching up and enjoying their meal, and Corbin promised Clementine that he would come visit more often in the future.

"I'm going to get your bag now. I can include those tea candies, too. Why don't you join Clementine for a tour," Belinda said to Corbin.

"Oh yes, let me show you around," Clementine said.

Corbin looked around the cottage and saw the herbs and items the two witches sold.

"I have really enjoyed my visit today, ladies, but I'm afraid I do have to get back to my pet snake," Corbin said.

"You have a pet snake?" Clementine asked.

"Yes, I do," Corbin replied.

"Oh, I'd love to meet him," Clementine said.

"Aww, okay, I can bring him next time I come," Corbin replied.

Corbin grabbed his items, said goodbye, and left. He had brought a fanny pack with him so he could store his items, and when he turned back into a raven, his items would not fall or get lost. Once he was back at the entrance of Ebony Woodlands, he turned back into a raven and flew away. When he had reached the cave where Cosmo was, it was still dark out, so he changed back into human form and headed inside quickly, closing the door he had built for the cave. He hoped to be able to use the location during future visits to the island.

***

The next morning, Corbin went outside and let Cosmo roam about in front of the river while he gathered some supplies for their new vacation home. Corbin found a coconut tree nearby and grabbed a few coconuts, which would last him a few weeks.

"I'll just put a non-rotting spell on these so they don't spoil. Let's go inside. We need to make the potion now that I have found the supplies I needed," Corbin said to Cosmo.

Corbin took the items out of his bag and set them up on a counter he had made inside the cave. Next, he started a fire and placed his cauldron on top of it. Although this cauldron was smaller than the one he had at home, it still worked enough to get the spell done. He began throwing items in and waited for the mix to start bubbling. Once there were bubbles, he began to read the spell aloud. Nothing happened the first time around, so he reread the spell, and again, nothing happened.

"Hmm, something's not right," Corbin said.

He grabbed his spell book and reread the instructions carefully. In fine print, down at the very bottom of the page, there was a note. *All of the above must be done in combination with mermaid dust.*

"Ugh! I knew it! It is a good thing I did not use all of my ingredients on this potion. I can still recreate it, but how do I get that mermaid dust, and where do I start looking?" Corbin asked Cosmo.

Cosmo hissed back at him, slithering around the countertop.

Corbin reached for his crystal ball and asked it where he could find the dust he was looking for. The crystal ball lit up and showed him Bryce.

"I knew it!" Corbin exclaimed. "I must now find Harper. If I find her, I'll find Bryce," Corbin said.

He gathered a few of his things and set off to find Harper and the pirates. He turned back into a raven, leaving Cosmo behind with food and water.

***

By this time, Harper and the pirates had reached the rainforest and were gathering some dragon fruits that they had discovered near the waterfall.

"What exactly are we looking for, Kellan?" Bryce asked.

"We need to find the code. We aren't far. It is just behind this waterfall. The space is covered by trees, limiting sunlight. Once we're inside, I'll explain everything," Kellan said.

"Oh, it's gorgeous! It is so lush, especially the green forest trees and plants," Harper said.

"I had a feeling you'd like it. It even has a willow tree like the one in the flower field," Kellan said.

The treehouse was built on an actual black redwood tree and was very sturdy. The outside was camouflaged to look like a regular tree, with leaves that draped down from the top of it, covering all of the roofing of the house. The treehouse also had plants that surrounded it, such as Japanese maples, spruce trees, western hemlocks, and mountain hemlocks, and they provided shade. The areas surrounding the treehouse was full of willow trees. There seemed to be around sixteen trees. Therefore, the leaves of the willow trees appeared to make curtains that went all the way around the treehouse. The only way inside was through the side entrance, which was near the waterfall where Harper and the crew had been gathering dragon fruits.

"Let's go inside," Kellan said.

Harper and the rest of the crew followed Kellan inside the treehouse and shut the door behind them. On the inside, the treehouse had been renovated and was very modern. There were soft gray tones throughout the house. It consisted of two bedrooms, a small one and a large one, and the entire house came with central air.

"Did you fix this place up?" Harper asked.

"Austin and I did, and we used some magic, as well," Kellan said. "This treehouse is where I decided to hide your treasures. They will be safe here. Right now, they are in your room, on your dresser."

"This treehouse really is a dream," Harper said, smiling.

"You must never reveal what it is outside of this space, or someone else will have access to it. Use the code outside of this space," Kendall said.

"Okay, I'll have to memorize that code," Harper replied.

Harper and Bryce looked around and noticed that on the small couch, there were sky-blue pillows, blankets, and robes. Harper picked one of the robes up and felt its incredibly soft material.

"What are these for, Kellan?" Harper asked.

"Those are so we can keep warm during the fall and winter months," Kellan said, referring to the blankets.

"I think she meant the robes," Bryce replied.

"Oh, right. Those are for traveling and for times of need. They will present themselves inside your bags if you ever need them while on the island," Kellan replied, grinning. "Shall we see the deck and yard?"

"Yes, I didn't know this house had a yard, especially considering the open space it is surrounded by," Bryce said.

"Yes, well, we have a yard so that Kobe has a place to sleep at night," Kellan said.

"Kobe? Who is Kobe?" Harper asked.

"He's half dachshund, half chihuahua. Although he is small, he is a fearless little guy and will protect you and Bryce, and he'll protect the house when you are away," Kellan said.

"The house also has features that allow him to play when no one is around. That way, he doesn't get lonely," Austin said.

"That's good to know. Amber is half dachshund, as well. She needs a friend, too. Maybe she will get to visit him someday," Harper said.

"Here he is. Hello, buddy," Austin said, petting Kobe.

"He's so cute. This yard is fairly big and has another doghouse. Is there another dog?" Harper asked.

"Oh yeah, I forgot to mention Shadow. He is half Siberian husky, half Akita, and he's also half magic. He will only appear during times when he is needed, such as if he needs to protect Kobe, Bryce, and you when you come back. He will guard the opening and will remain outside the treehouse." Kellan said, and then he turned to Kobe. "Okay, bye, buddy. We will be back. Be a good boy for Shadow."

Kellan closed the door that led to the yard. The pirates followed Harper into her room so that they could see what other items she had found during her previous travels.

"Now that we're here, can you show us what you and Bryce found? We have to start heading back soon, and you should leave behind other items that you want keep safe," Kendall said.

"Okay, let me add the rest of the treasure to the safe. We need to get one with a lock," Harper said.

"Okay, I can pick one up at my parents' place and bring it here. I'll transfer the items from the current safe to the one with the lock," Kellan said.

"Sounds like a plan to me, but you're not going alone," Harper said.

"You can meet me here. You can bring Bryce and your cousin if you'd like," Kellan said.

"Oh, Kelsey can come? Okay, we will be here next Thursday. Kelsey won't be here until then," Harper said.

"Okay, fair enough," Kellan replied.

After Harper had put the treasures away and locked the treehouse, she headed back to the Black Mist with the crew. They walked until they reached the same lake they had crossed on the way to the rainforest.

"We need to stop here for food and water again," Bryce said.

"Okay, you all can fuel up. I'll keep watch. I think I ate too much earlier, anyway," Mr. Nomad said.

The crew sat within a circle of giant rocks that hid them from sight.

"It's a good thing we picked all of those dragon fruits earlier," Austin said.

"We'll have food on the ship on the way back. This is only a snack break," Kendall said.

"Oh, good. I could really use some heavy carbs right about now," Bryce said, grinning.

"Don't worry, lad. I have something in mind that will fix all of you right up," Mr. Nomad said.

When the crew had eaten the dragon fruits and refilled the water flasks, they continued to walk until they got to the coast of the island.

"We have company. Let's get back on the Black Mist before they get back to their ship," Captain Dawson said.

The crew got on the Black Mist and prepared to set sail again. The same spell that brought them onto the island needed to be said so they could get back off of the island.

"Grab ahold of something," Bruce shouted.

"We're going down," Captain Dawson yelled.

Harper grabbed Kellan's hand as she strapped herself to a post with rope. The Black Mist then began to sink, slowly at first, and then it gradually got faster as it got closer the surface. Once in the open ocean again, the pirates prepared to head back to Sterling Krystalline.

"Can you help me get untied," Harper said to Kellan, letting go of his hand.

"Yes, Princess. I'm starving. I hope Mr. Nomad can dry the kitchen off in a short period of time so we can eat soon. I'll go help him, and you can get dried off," Kellan said.

"Okay, that sounds like a good idea," Harper said.

Harper had packed some extra clothes in her bag and had made sure she had placed them in a giant Ziplock bag before they headed for Isla Mordaz. She went into the room she had been staying in, inside the captain's quarters, and looked in one of the drawers. Water came spilling out of the drawer. Her bag was floating on top of the water, but it was zipped tight in the Ziplock bag. When she opened the bag, her mini backpack was dry, and so were the other items inside it, including her clothes. She put her wet clothes in the Ziplock bag, and after drying it off she placed it inside her mini backpack. She put her mini backpack on and headed toward the front deck.

"Food's almost ready! I can't wait!" Bryce said to Harper.

"What are we having?" Harper asked.

"Captain's favorite. Fish, chips, and popcorn shrimp," Bryce said.

"We get all of that?" Harper asked aloud.

"Yes, you do! And a side of coleslaw, too. We will be having bubbly water and some warm cheese biscuits as a starter. Why don't you both head to the captain's quarters to sit and wait with the rest of the crew," Mr. Nomad replied, smiling.

"Okay, let's go, Harper," Bryce said.

Later, when the pirates were seated, Mr. Nomad, Bruce, and Barton served the food in the center of the table. The main dishes were popcorn shrimp and crisp golden fish. The side dishes were fresh-cut potato chips and fried kale. A bowl of tomatoes, lemon, cilantro, onion, and radish was placed next to it, along with a dish that held cheese biscuits.

"Dig in, everyone. I know you must all be very hungry," Captain Dawson said.

Harper, Bryce, and the pirates ate the meal and talked about what they had experienced on the island.

"So, how did you come across this island?" Harper asked Kellan.

"My father. He was the one who told me about it. He said that if I should ever need a place of refuge, I should go there. I then made the decision to share it with you and Bryce," Kellan said.

"We are grateful to both of you," Harper said.

"Yes, and thank you for cooking, Mr. Nomad! The meal was delicious!" Bryce said.

"If anyone has room for dessert, I made crème brûlée," Mr. Nomad said.

"That is my favorite. Have you topped them with berries? Can we also get some tea, please?" Kendall said.

"Of course, and yes, you can choose from peach or pomegranate," Mr. Nomad replied.

"I'll have peach, please," Kendall said.

"I'll have pomegranate, please," Harper said.

"Me, too. Pomegranate sounds good," Bryce said.

"Okay, I have placed the tea in the middle of the table. The red mugs are pomegranate, and the orange mugs are peach. Help yourselves," Mr. Nomad replied.

"Land ahead. We're almost home, Harper!" Captain Dawson said.

"That means we're about an hour away," Austin said.

"Thanks for the update, Captain," Harper said.

After she finished her dessert and tea, Harper walked onto the deck and stared out at the open ocean. The icy-cold wind in her hair and the sounds of seagulls flying above her felt like a dream.

"What's on your mind?" Bryce asked after coming out to join her.

"Not much. I'm actually pretty tired, but I'm really glad I was able to take this journey, and I hope it won't be our last," Harper replied.

"Maybe we can bring Kelsey on our next adventure," Bryce said, blushing.

"Of course! I think she will like being out with us," Harper replied.

"I think I'll ask Kellan, too," Bryce said.

"Wait a minute. You like her, don't you?" Harper said.

"Maybe," Bryce replied, grinning.

"It's all over your face, mate. Don't try to deny it," Kellan said suddenly.

"How long were you standing there?" Bryce asked.

"Long enough, and yes, Kelsey can join us next time. It appears we have made it to Sterling Krystalline safely. I believe this is where you both depart. Captain Dawson has arranged a ride from the beach to the palace, Princess," Kellan said.

Harper went down into the captain's quarters, grabbed her things, said goodbye to the crew, and gave Kellan a hug before she and Bryce got off the Black Mist. They both waved goodbye as the pirates sailed off, heading back out into the ocean.

"I'll see you in the morning, Princess," Bryce said.

"Okay, let's make it a beach day," Harper said, waving.

A carriage picked Harper up and took her straight to the palace. On the way there, Harper began to think about how the captain had arranged a ride for her, so she asked her driver, "How did you know to pick me up? We were at sea for a couple of days, so I'm just curious."

"The captain spoke to me about keeping you safe after he met you at one of your balls. I was paid by him to make sure you always have a way home. The name is Spencer. I was already working for the king before that, though. I was referred by Kelsey, my best friend," she said.

"Kelsey? She's my cousin," Harper replied.

"Really? Well, it was definitely a pleasure meeting you and serving you, Princess. Have a good night," Spencer said.

Harper got down from the carriage and closed the door. She walked into the manor and found Amber waiting for her. Harper picked her up, gave her kisses, and walked with her to the back yard, where her parents were having tea. She sat and played with Amber for a while before going up to her bedroom, showering, and going to bed. She was tired and fell asleep within minutes of lying down. She slept for nine hours straight and awoke the next day to the sound of rain falling. After she had gotten ready for the day, she grabbed her bag and went downstairs.

"I'm going to see Bryce. I've got my raincoat," Harper shouted out loud.

"Be careful in the rain," Harper's mother shouted back.

""Okay," Harper said.

Harper closed the door behind her and locked it, then headed toward the beach. The rain had gotten lighter and felt like a steady drizzle. When she arrived at the beach, she spotted Bryce sitting on the shore.

"Hey, I love this weather!" Harper said to Bryce.

"I didn't think you would come. For a second, it looked like it would be getting worse," Bryce said.

"A little rain wasn't going to stop me," Harper replied.

"I was looking for the X again, but it's gone. I'm not sure what happened to it," Bryce said.

"I think it only appears when it has clues for us, or when it feels there is information for us to know," Harper said.

"An X would know all that?" Bryce asked.

"No, silly, I meant magic. But I feel like we will never find this other ring. Where could it be?" Harper said, spreading her body across the sand.

"Well, try to be positive. Have faith. It's taking longer than we expected or wanted, but we will find it. You'll see. Just not right now," Bryce replied with a smile.

"How can you be so sure?" Harper said.

"I can't, but that's where faith comes in," Bryce said.

The rain had gotten heavier, and the clouds turned black above the two friends.

"Look above us. There is a storm coming. I hope you packed for another adventure," Bryce said.

"I am always ready. I just didn't tell my parents I'd be gone this long, but I think they'll figure it out. Where are we heading?" Harper asked.

"Look, the pirates are back. Let's get a lift from them. Maybe it's time to really explore Isla Mordaz," Bryce said.

"All right," Harper said.

"Kellan, down here! Do you have room for us?" Bryce shouted as the wind blew against his hair.

"Yes! Give me your hand," Kellan said.

"Hold on to me," Bryce said to Harper.

Harper grabbed ahold of Bryce, and Bryce grabbed ahold of Kellan, who lifted them both with Kendall's fairy dust, then set them down on the Black Mist.

"I'll warn you now that we won't be returning until the storm has passed," Kellan said to Harper and Bryce.

"Okay, we figured," Harper said.

"Toward the maelstrom, then," Kellan said.

"Nonsense, boy! Do not say that. We don't wish to be cursed that way. We will be passing it slowly, and we might take refuge on a nearby island depending on how bad it gets," Captain Dawson said.

***

Meanwhile, Corbin had made his way back from Isla Mordaz and was with Cosmo inside their dungeon. He was now growing impatient over not knowing Harper's whereabouts. He went into his closet and looked for his crystal ball.

"Show me where the princess is," Corbin said aloud.

The crystal ball revealed Harper's location and showed Corbin that she was aboard the Black Mist, riding with the pirates in the ocean.

"Well, well, if trouble is what they seek, then trouble is what they will get. *Crystal ball that tells all, create a maelstrom in the Black Mist's path so that I can show them my wrath*," Corbin said aloud.

***

Suddenly, the storm grew worse on the ocean, and a maelstrom formed before the Black Mist and its crew.

"Oh no! Look what you've done. Watch your words next time," Austin said to Kellan.

"Me? I have not done anything, although I will consider which words I use next time. Look out! Austin, tell Captain Dawson there is another ship on the horizon, right behind the maelstrom. It appears to be black, aqua, and orange, and it has gray lettering," Kellan said.

"Those colors are really bright, mate! All hands on deck," Austin shouted.

Kendall looked into her spyglass and saw that Kellan was right. Why hadn't they seen this ship before? She was sure she would not have missed it. How could she, especially with those colors?

"They aren't here to help us. They are an enemy ship. Prepare the cannons. We're both heading into the center of the maelstrom, and with the rain I can't sprinkle pixie dust onto the Black Mist to make it fly," Kendall said before turning to the captain. "Captain Dawson, do you know who they are?"

"Apparently, it's the Autumn Corpse. Look on the ship's bow," Captain Dawson replied.

On the front of the Autumn Corpse, there was a skull that resembled a pumpkin in the center of a maple leaf, and there was a smaller one on the rear of the ship, as well. It almost seemed as if the ship was meant to represent Halloween. The crew on this ship consisted of seven pirates, including Captain Hamish Connors, Blaze Park, Keaton Stone, Lola Lawrence, Garret Vons, Vince Perry, and Vick Watson. Part of the crew knew Corbin and were good friends with him, which meant they knew the Black Mist was an opponent, not an ally.

Harper grabbed a spyglass and looked through it, then exclaimed, "How could they have gotten here so fast?"

"They didn't! Magic brought them here through a portal," Bryce replied.

"But who cast the spell?" Harper asked.

"Let me see that spyglass," Bryce said.

As he looked for signs of who could be behind the attack, he saw the other crew preparing to fire with their cannons, so he exclaimed, "Head for the cannons. They're going to shoot!"

Harper and Bryce ran behind Austin and Mr. Nomad, heading toward the cannons. They loaded them and prepared to shoot.

"We're still not close enough," Mr. Nomad said.

"Bryce, I know its Corbin!" Harper said.

"What? How do you know that? Why do you think that?" Bryce replied.

"I don't know. I just have a feeling!" Harper said.

"Arguing over the subject won't help, Corbin or not," Austin replied.

"We're going to have to go through it!" Bruce said.

"No, we can go around it! I can see Python Cove from here. We can take refuge there!" Kellan said.

"No, we can't! The Autumn Corpse crew will see us and follow. But we can go around them," Barton said.

"But that's impossible!" Bryce replied.

"All things are possible. The word separated says 'I'm possible!' To achieve what seems impossible, one has to first believe that it is possible. It may look different than you want it to, and it may be scary, but that doesn't mean you can't overcome it. Keep the faith, mate," Kellan said.

"I need you boys to buy me some time. I'm going to look for a spell in my book of spells. Keep the ships from intertwining and shoot the cannons. They've started their attack!" Kendall said.

"You've got it!" Austin replied. "Get ready to shoot, Bruce and Barton!"

"Aye aye, mate!" Bruce and Barton replied.

"My reverse spell should work for this. Help me look in my closet. It's in the captain's quarters," Kendall said to Harper.

"Okay," Harper replied.

They both went to the captain's quarters and searched the closet until they came across a navy chest. Harper opened the lid and saw the spell book.

"I found it," Harper said.

"Great work. Now, let's see here," Kendall said, flipping through the pages of the book. "Here it is!"

They ran back to the deck, and Kendall exclaimed, "Harper, Bryce, Austin, and Kellan, repeat after me! Power over ocean, wind, maelstrom, and crew, I command you to blow away the storm and send it back to the master who sent it out! Say it again. Louder! All together!"

After the crew had repeated this several times, they waited to see if it would work. After three minutes, the approaching ship and crew were gone, but the maelstrom remained.

"This can't be. We need to get away from the maelstrom," Kendall said.

"What are we going to do now?" Harper asked.

As Harper's mind raced, the ship grew closer and closer to the maelstrom. Suddenly, she remembered the black book of spells that her father had given her when she was younger.

"Only use this book if you are ever in trouble, and only as a last resort," King Henry said Harper's memory.

Harper reached into her pocket and found the book. She opened it and looked inside, finding a spell that could potentially rescue them. She quickly read the spell aloud, saying, *"'All the powers of Earth, come unto me. Bring forth a fierce creature from the past, one from the land and sea. Come unto me, Jurassic survivors that are able to withstand dangers of great magnitude. Mother Nature, come unto me. Bestow upon me this wish until dusk and then take back the hands of time and rewind, answering my want. Then let death tear them apart.'"*

Shortly after Harper had repeated the spell, she saw what looked like a large bird flying toward their ship.

"What have you done?" Kendall shouted.

"Trust me," Harper replied.

As it got closer, the crew saw the enormous Quetzalcoatlus northropi. This dinosaur was half pelican (top half), half pterodactyl (bottom half). The huge bird circled the ship, landing on one of its sails. It tried to fly away with the ship but failed.

"He needs my help. He can't do it alone, but I can't help him! It's still raining!" Kendall said.

Before Harper could reply, she saw another dinosaur appear in the water, and she shouted, "Look! It's a brachiosaurus!"

Chapter Three

Python Cove

The brachiosaurus began to push the ship, helping the Quetzalcoatlus northropi shift the weight of the ship. The Quetzalcoatlus northropi flew in the opposite direction of the storm, helping the brachiosaurus swim and push the ship away from the maelstrom, and Captain Dawson steered the ship toward Python Cove. Python Cove was an island where pirates and sailors went to rest or restock on food, water, gunpowder, or any other supplies they needed for their ships. The island got its name because it was famous for housing all different types of snakes, and the native people of the island had built a restaurant and resort for visitors to make money. There were also tours for people who were interested in seeing the different kinds of snakes, and those tours could be booked in the summer on a first-come-first-serve basis. The island was also rumored to have hidden gems and artifacts, but it was hidden by all different types of tropical plants as well as rocks as black as night, so the island could easily be missed by pirates or sailors who had not yet discovered its location.

As Harper stared into the ocean, she saw sparkles and shouted, "Kendall, can you use the pixie dust yet?"

"Not yet. It's still pouring," Kendall shouted back.

Desperate to get the ship to move away from the maelstrom, Harper closed her eyes and began to pray for a miracle. When she opened her eyes after five minutes, she saw the water beneath them begin to change colors.

"Look in the water, Kendall!" Harper exclaimed.

Kendall looked in the water and saw sparkles underneath the ship.

"We're moving toward the island, but the brachiosaurus is gone," Kendall said aloud.

"How do you know? What is moving us?" Harper asked.

"It's a hippocampus, and she's gorgeous. I knew he was gone the second the ship felt lighter," Kellan replied.

The hippocampus had aqua-colored hair and white-colored skin, and there were sparkles along its body that looked like aqua pixie dust in the light. The hippocampus had magic that could move the ship in the direction it moved.

"The hippocampi are rare. They only appear to those who believe in them and really need their help. You wished for it, didn't you?" Kellan asked Harper.

"It seems your faith is stronger than you thought," Kendall said.

Harper smiled.

The ship began to get closer to Python Cove. The rain had gotten lighter and felt more like a light drizzle. The Q, which is what Kellan called the flying dinosaur, had flown away and disappeared shortly after he realized the brachiosaurus knew what direction to take the ship, and once the Black Mist was close enough to Python Cove, the hippocampus also disappeared. The Black Mist arrived at Python Cove in the late afternoon, and

Kendall sent the crew out for water, food, toiletries, gunpowder, and weapons. They would need the weapons if they encountered another enemy ship.

"We'll stay at Snakes Inn tonight. We're all checked in. Follow me," Kellan said.

Harper and Bryce followed Kellan into the motel. The inside of the motel was full of snake decorations, and there was a lot of attention to detail both inside and outside the rooms they were staying in. Each room had a snake in a cage, and each room had a different colored snake.

"Is that why they call this island Python Cove?" Bryce asked Kellan.

"Yes and no. Are you scared of snakes?" Kellan asked, laughing.

"Yes, I am," Bryce replied.

"I love snakes! I am absolutely in love with this island so far!" Harper said as she stared at the green python inside the cage in her room.

"You'll love the drinks here, too. The virgin piña coladas are amazing! They have four different combinations. The food here is fairly good, too, but I suppose you'll find that out during dinner," Kellan replied.

"Why couldn't we stay on the ship again?" Bryce asked.

"Cheer up, mate. We all wanted a break. The snakes will not hurt you. Stay close. You will be fine. In thirty minutes, we are meeting Kendall and the rest of the crew at the restaurant inside the inn," Kellan said.

Once they had changed clothes and freshened up, Kellan, Harper, and Bryce headed toward the restaurant.

"What is this place called?" Bryce asked.

"Snakes Tavern," Kellan replied.

"There they are," Harper said, pointing to the rest of crew.

Once they were seated, the waiter (a black-and-navy medusa) stopped by the table and hissed, saying, "We will serve water as well as chips and salsa. This on the house. If you wish to order additional drinks, please look at our drink menu."

"Thank you," Kendall said.

"Are you serious? Thanks for mentioning the waiter is a snake!" Bryce said as the waiter walked away.

"Ha! Relax. After all, we're at Python Cove. What did you expect? Their everywhere here," Kellan replied.

"What's good here aside from the drinks?" Harper asked Kellan.

"I love their edamame and fried tofu. The combo comes with fresh ginger," Kellan replied.

"Good choice. I think I'll have that and a virgin piña colada," Harper said.

"I'll have the same," Bryce said.

"Waiter, I think we're ready," Austin said.

Once the waiter had come back to the table and the pirates had ordered, Harper got up to look around. It seemed very tropical inside the restaurant, almost like a rainforest full of snakes. She was intrigued by the snakes and liked staring at the differences in color and shape.

"Princess, can I join you?" Kellan asked.

"Sure," Harper said.

Kellan followed Harper into a hallway that was decorated with trees. The hallway led to a room that turned into a cave, and Harper's curiosity grew, so she continued to explore the room. The ceilings were decorated differently in every room.

There were stars, skies, and treasures depicting snakes from different myths.

"This place is magical," Harper said.

"Yeah, it is," Kellan replied as he walked closer to her.

Kellan gazed up at the details for a few moments, then looked back down at Harper's eyes. When she caught him staring at her, she got closer to his face and stared back, leaning in slowly. Closing their eyes, their lips touched, and they both began to kiss passionately. It had only been three minutes when Bryce came looking for them.

"There you are. The food's…ready," Bryce said, with his jaw dropping as he saw them kissing.

Bryce left the room and sat back down at the table.

"What's wrong? You look like you have seen a ghost. Too many snakes for you?" Bruce asked, laughing.

"Did you tell Harper her food was here?" Barton asked.

"Uh, yeah. I think she's busy," Bryce replied.

Bryce's entrance had not startled Kellan or Harper, and they continued to kiss. They eventually joined everyone back at the table.

"Where did you both disappear to?" Austin asked.

"She wanted to see the snake room's details, right, Harper?" Kellan asked.

"Yes, I did. They are amazing," Harper said.

"I see you chose a different drink than me. What is it?" Harper asked Kellan.

"It's a virgin strawberry daiquiri. Do you want to try it?" Kellan replied.

"Sure, I'll try it," Harper said, taking the drink. "Wow, these are both really good. I think I prefer the strawberries, though."

"Do you wish to trade? I think I prefer the pineapple anyway," Kellan said.

"Okay," Harper replied.

"How do you like the food, Harper?" Captain Dawson asked.

"It is really good. They have great flavors here. I think taste is always better than quantity," Harper replied.

"That's good to hear," Captain Dawson said.

"They have dancing here?" Bryce asked Barton.

"Oh yeah, I've heard they have it every night. Will you be joining them?" Barton asked.

"Yeah, why not? I'll give it a go," Bryce said.

After they had finished their meals, half of the crew went back to gather materials for the ship, and the other half stayed inside the restaurant for a night of dancing. Bryce was popular with the girls, and so was Barton. Meanwhile, Harper and Kellan danced with each other.

"He looks like he's been bewitched by her," Barton said to Bryce, watching Harper and Kellan dance.

"I think he may be," Bryce replied.

***

Back on the dance floor, Harper and Kellan continued to dance, and as Bryce, Bruce, and Barton began to get farther away from them, Kellan stared into Harper's eyes.

"Are we going to talk? I don't want it to be awkward," Kellan said softly to Harper.

"It's not awkward. I think we should wait until we have another 'moment' like we did back there in the snake room," Harper replied.

"I agree. Forgive me if I pushed the limits of your boundaries," Kellan replied.

"You don't need to apologize. Let's move on. It happened, and I'd be lying if I said I didn't like it, but now isn't the right time to pursue whatever this may be. We have other things to chase after right now. We need that ring, and we can't lose focus," Harper said.

"Okay, fair enough. Let's at least pretend for the others that nothing happened," Kellan said.

"Very well," Harper agreed.

Kellan and Harper continued to dance until an old friend of Kellan's showed up.

"Blaze?" Kellan said, walking over to the bar.

"Hey, Kellan, what are you doing here?" Blaze asked.

"My ship stopped at this island to refuel," Kellan replied.

"Oh, what are the odds? So did mine," Blaze said.

"Really? I didn't even know you had joined a crew," Kellan said.

"I did last time I was here. The Autumn Corpse crew was recruiting, and they had a sign-up list. I signed it, and they chose me to join them," Blaze said.

"Well, it was very nice running into you, lad, but it's time for us to go," Kellan said, and then he walked back over to Harper. "It's time to go. Go grab our stuff. Take Bryce, Bruce, and Barton and head out to the Black Mist. I'll meet all four of you there," Kellan said in a low tone.

Harper was a little confused, but she did as Kellan had said, heading over to Bryce, grabbing his hand, and saying, "We have to go now."

"Okay. Barton, we're leaving. Let's go," Bryce said, grabbing Barton's arm.

Barton grabbed Bruce's arm, and the four of them headed toward the inn, where they had left their belongings, then headed to the Black Mist. Once they were done loading their things, Captain Dawson and the rest of the crew boarded the ship.

"We're ready for takeoff. Next stop is Isla Mordaz," Captain Dawson said.

"Where are Kellan and Kendall? We can't leave without them," Austin said.

"They'll catch up. The Autumn Corpse crew has found Python Cove. We can't stay. If we do, we risk being recognized, and Kellan knows someone on their crew already," Mr. Nomad replied.

The Black Mist was beginning to sail away from Python Cove when Kendall and Kellan reached the dock.

"Get ready to fly," Kendall said.

She reached for her pixie dust, grabbed Kellan's hand, and jumped off the dock and into the air. Spreading their arms out, the two followed the Black Mist, flying after it. Once the ship had sailed far away enough away from the island, Captain Dawson slowed the speed of the ship, allowing Kellan and Kendall to land on the deck and make their way to the captain's quarters.

"That was a close call. I wasn't expecting Blaze to be part of the Autumn Corpse crew," Kellan said.

"Yeah, well, at least now you know, and we got away. On another topic, what happened with you and Harper back at the restaurant?" Kendall asked Kellan.

"I had a moment of weakness. I won't be letting that get in my way in the future," Kellan replied.

"I think I know what happened. Your time will come. Get to know her better," Kendall said.

Kellan grinned and then went back up the deck to join the others.

Meanwhile, Harper had gone into her room on the ship and was sitting on her bed with Bryce.

"What happened back there? And don't lie to me!" Bryce asked Harper.

"I had a moment of weakness. I won't be letting that get in my way in the future," Harper replied.

"What is that supposed to mean! Harper, you sound like you regret it, and I know you don't. Why are you so opposed to the idea of him? Because he's not a prince? Because he's a pirate?" Bryce asked.

"Maybe," Harper replied.

"Give him a chance and get to know him better. If not for yourself, do it to prove me wrong," Bryce said.

"All right, but only because you asked me to," Harper replied as she hugged him. "I'm glad you're my best friend. Otherwise, talking about this would have been so awkward."

They both laughed.

***

When the pirates arrived where the island of Mordaz normally was, they saw the rock formation, but it looked different. The rocks were in a straight line instead of the circle they normally formed around the island. The pirates circled the area and found nothing but open ocean.

"Where is it, Bryce? It couldn't have just disappeared into thin air, could it?" Harper asked Bryce.

"Maybe we're just lost," Bryce replied.

"Give me the dust," Harper said.

"No, Harper, you can't leave the ship alone. I'm coming with you," Bryce said.

After they had sprinkled pixie dust on their legs, they jumped into the water and began to swim, looking for hints of where the island could be. After diving deeper into the ocean, Harper froze in her tracks when she came face to face with a great white shark. Before she had a chance to react, she saw a cave in the distance. It was one she recognized from before, and it was almost as if it had appeared out of thin air. She signed to Bryce, who was waiting behind the shark, and they both swam for the cave. The great white followed them and was getting close, but then it crashed into the rocks that surrounded part of the cave, sinking to the bottom of the ocean.

"Is he gone?" Bryce asked.

"Yes, I think so. Let's get back up to the shore," Harper said.

Once they had swum up to the surface, they grabbed on to the Black Mist and sprinkled the dust from the magic shell on their tails. After they had their feet back, they both climbed onto the ship.

"Did you find anything?" Barton asked.

"No, the island is gone," Bryce replied.

"Look in the distance. It's the Autumn Corpse," Kellan shouted.

"What are they doing here?" Kendall asked.

"They must have followed us, or maybe they are looking for the island, too. But why?" Harper said.

"Corbin!" Kellan and Harper said at the same time.

Kellan grinned and walked over to where Harper was, then said, "I had a hunch."

"Me, too. I think the island has disappeared because it senses we're in danger. We have to come back at another time," Harper said.

"Aye aye, Princess," Kellan replied, and Harper blushed. "Captain, land ho!"

"Where can we go from here? If the Autumn Corpse crew doesn't find what they are looking for, they will return to Python Cove," Kendall said.

"There is another island not far from here. It's about an hour north. Grab the compass and check where we are. We can stay there for the night," Austin said to Bruce.

Bruce did as Austin said and helped the captain steer the ship in that direction.

Chapter Four

Skerry Moor

"What is this island called?" Barton asked.

"Skerry Moor," Austin replied.

Skerry Moor was an island of mosses, and it was covered in coral reefs and an abundance of mossy trees that came in various shades of green, yellow, and purple. The only inn on the island had been built from wood and was covered in moss, which helped it camouflage into its surroundings.

The pirates had gathered in the pirates' quarters for some peach tea as Captain Dawson continued to steer the ship. Mr. Nomad had volunteered to keep him company and had served him some tea in a Tervis. While they warmed up with the tea, Austin began to tell the crew about the island.

"This island is smaller than Python Cove. The people are known for using rich-tasting coconuts for food and water. Before I joined the Black Mist crew, I spotted this island. I think you will enjoy its beauty. Although they aren't the most liked creatures, this island is home to the banana slug. They come in different colors and shapes," Austin said.

"It sounds different. What's the weather like there?" Harper asked.

"It is a little warmer than what you're used to, the highest being seventy-eight degrees," Austin said.

"That's not too bad. How long will be staying?" Bryce asked.

"Well, tonight, and then we will leave at one p.m. tomorrow and see if we can still stop by Isla Mordaz," Austin said.

The different colors of mosses on the island made it appealing to its visitors. The trees formed arches, creating a roof for some of the homes and the inn on the moor. When the pirates got there, it was late, and part of the crew was hungry.

"How can we hide the Black Mist? It's not exactly camouflaged," Captain Dawson said to Austin.

"See that area next to the island? There are moss trees that form shelter on the water. The people here use it to store things they don't want others to find. Since it is very dark, no one will ever suspect there is anything inside, especially since it is in the middle of the island. People put broken tree branches and logs at the entrance to give the elution that there is nothing inside." Austin replied, shining his flashlight in that direction.

"All right, I'll take the ship and hide it after you all get off," Captain Dawson said.

"No, let me do it, or you'll have to swim back to shore," Kendall said.

"We can both go. It's far too dark for you to go alone," Captain Dawson said.

Once Kendall and Captain Dawson had hidden the Black Mist and rejoined the crew, they all checked into the inn. At the front counter, they were greeted by a non-winged fairy, who smiled and said, "How can I help you?"

"We'd like to stay the night at your inn," Austin replied.

"Okay, for how many?" the fairy replied.

"Nine, please," Mr. Nomad said.

"Okay, follow me, please," the fairy said, grabbing a pre-lit lantern.

The fairy had long pink hair and bright-blue eyes. She had lavender clothing and nails. The crew followed her into the forest, which was dimly lit by fireflies.

"Here we are. This inn was designed to hold up to one hundred guests, and it is one of three that we have on the moor. You will be in room nineteen. It has space for up to twenty guests and is one of our bigger rooms. If you need anything, please let one of the winged fairies know," she said, handing Austin the key, and then she left to go back to the front counter.

The winged fairies were younger than those without wings. The wings on the fairies who were working at the inn were large, and each set had its own unique details. The wings were also different colors; the color depended on a fairy's personality.

Austin opened the door, and inside the crew found a total of twenty bedrooms, each with their own door and restroom.

"I'll take the first one. I am so tired," Captain Dawson said.

"I call the purple room," Harper said.

"I'll take a purple one, too," Kendall said.

"I'm taking the green one next to the captain's," Kellan said.

"Cool, that means Bruce, Barton, Mr. Nomad, and I get all of the blue rooms," Bryce said.

"On second thought, I think I'm going to go check on the ship," Captain Dawson said, heading out of the inn.

"Um, okay. More like, 'I'm going to go talk to the fairy I met at the counter,'" Kellan said.

"Kellan! I mean, he could have wanted to check on the Black Mist, too, right?" Austin said, laughing.

"False," Kellan replied.

"Goodnight, everyone," Mr. Nomad said.

While the pirates were changing into different clothes for the night, Captain Dawson was walking over to see the fairy they had met at the counter.

"Hello, I was wondering if I could have some tea in my room," Captain Dawson said.

"That is what the winged fairies are for," the non-winged fairy replied.

"Oh, well, they weren't around, and to be honest, I had to see you again. Do you have a name?" Captain Dawson asked.

"My name is Heidi," the fairy replied.

"Heidi. That's a pretty name. Will you have tea with me tonight?" Captain Dawson asked.

"I'd like that, but who will watch the counter?" Heidi replied.

"We don't have to go anywhere. I'm okay with chatting right here. I see you have a tea pot at your workspace already. Can I make the tea for you?" Captain Dawson asked.

"Very well," Heidi said.

Captain Dawson made the tea and sat down to talk.

"Have you always lived here on Skerry Moor?" Captain Dawson asked.

"Yes, I was born and raised here. I do not have any siblings, but my parents were rulers of this land when they were alive. They had me at an older age and died a few years ago," Heidi replied.

"I'm sorry for your loss," Captain Dawson said.

"Thank you. I know they are watching over me, and I visit their burial site in the forest every Sunday. I like to pick the lilies in the field nearby to use as decorations, and I enchant them so that they can float over every grave. I have been watching over the graveyard since their deaths, and I've rearranged a lot of things on the grounds. I have a team of fairies who help me keep up with the maintenance. What about you? How did you become a pirate?" Heidi said.

"I was adopted when I was younger, and my adoptive parents owned a ship. They made it as a cruise so they could make money and show people some fun, touristic places in Britain. When I turned twenty, they decided to take a cruise for just the two of them, and they told me they would be away for a few days. A week went by, and I began to worry. They had not returned, so I asked around the marketplace to see if anyone had a rowboat I could borrow so I could set off to sea alone. I thought I was lost, but then I came across an island that was surrounded by sharks and spotted their ship. I jumped into the water and climbed aboard, but the ship was abandoned, and I never found their bodies or heard from them again. So, I took the ship and headed back home, then started using the ship to take short trips out to sea so I could search for them. During that time, I discovered Python Cove, and that's where I met my crew, and well, the rest is history," Captain Dawson said.

"I am so sorry about your parents!" Heidi replied.

"Thank you," Captain Dawson said.

They continued to talk about similarities and differences between them, and their conversation never seemed to reach an end. When morning came, Heidi put a closed sign up, thanked Captain Dawson for the tea, said goodbye, and went back to her house to get some rest. By the time Captain Dawson got back to the room, the crew members had already started their day and were getting ready to have breakfast in the dining area of their room.

"Well, well, look who made it back to join us," Austin said.

"Wow, you were up all night, weren't you?" Kellan said, shaking his head.

"Goodnight, ladies and gents," Captain Dawson said, grinning.

"Great, we aren't leaving here till late afternoon now, if that," Barton said.

"Let him sleep, or that will be our fate," Bruce said, laughing.

"So, what are we having today?" Harper asked

"We must request coconuts from the winged fairies. I'll do it," Kendall said, and then she walked outside and asked one of the winged fairies for the coconuts.

"I'll knock on your door when I have them all," the fairy said.

"Thank you," Kendall replied.

Kendall went back into the room and let the crew know their food and drinks were on the way.

"I think I like that you can only order one thing to eat," Harper said.

"I don't. Where is the meat?" Bryce replied.

"Same!" Austin said.

There was a knock on the door minutes later, and the winged fairy came in, smiled, and said, "Here is your order. We provided utensils so you can crack the coconuts open, and the drinks have straws in them already. Enjoy!"

"Thank you!" everyone in the crew said as she left.

After they had opened the coconuts with the utensils that had been provided, they all scooped up pieces of coconut with spoons and ate them.

"Wow, this is surprisingly really good," Bryce said.

"Yes, I love it. The water is surprisingly cold, as well, considering it doesn't have ice," Harper said.

The crew continued to enjoy the meal, and they talked and got to know each other better. The friendships between the pirates and Harper and Bryce grew deeper as they continued to spend time together. When they were done with breakfast, they set out to explore the moor. The trees provided shade during the day, making walks enjoyable, and the walks were interesting because of the different colors.

***

When Captain Dawson woke up from his nap, it was midafternoon. He quickly got ready for the day and headed back to the counter to check out.

"Hey, how'd you sleep, beautiful?" he asked Heidi.

"I slept well, thank you," she said, blushing.

"Can you please check me and my crew out. I'm afraid we have to go in a few minutes. We're headed back out on our quest," Captain Dawson said.

"Are you planning on leaving and not returning again?" Heidi asked, looking sad.

"I'll be back. Cheer up, doll," he said.

After she had checked them out, she gave him a hug. Before she could let go, Captain Dawson looked into her eyes and kissed her passionately. As they were kissing, Austin walked in and said, "Kendall and I are going to get the Black Mist. We'll be back to pick you up since you're busy," and then he left.

"I'll be back to see you," Captain Dawson said.

"I'm hopeful, and I trust you're a man of your word," Heidi said.

After they had said goodbye, Captain Dawson headed toward the Black Mist, but he ran into Austin and Kendall, who had gotten the Black Mist and had come back to get the crew.

"Were taking off," Austin said.

The crew got on the ship, and Captain Dawson followed.

"Ready for takeoff, lover boy?" Austin asked, teasing.

"All hands on deck," Captain Dawson said, grinning.

They left Skerry Moore after prepping the Black Mist for takeoff, and the crew got hungry after only an hour onboard.

Chapter Five

Return to Isla Mordaz

Mr. Nomad had known they would be hungry, so he had decided to start cooking before they could say anything.

"Who's hungry?" Austin asked.

"Me!" everyone in the crew replied.

"I knew that was coming," Mr. Nomad said.

"What's on the menu this afternoon?" Kellan asked, smiling.

"Shrimp skewers and rice pilaf, along with garlic bread squares, roasted broccoli, and ice water," Mr. Nomad said.

"Oh man, that sounds amazing! I don't think I could live on coconuts alone," Austin said.

"Of course, you couldn't," Kendall said, kissing him.

"Food will be ready in thirty minutes," Mr. Nomad said.

"Let's go set up the captain's quarters," Kendall said to Harper and Bryce.

The three of them headed inside and set the table for their upcoming meal. After they finished, Mr. Nomad and the rest of the crew came in with the food.

"I'm ready to dive in," Bryce said.

"Help yourselves, mates. There's a plate with lemon, as well, for your convenience," Mr. Nomad said.

"This is so good, as always. You outdid yourself, Mr. Nomad," Harper said.

"I'm glad you like it, dear, but I think we were all starved after having coconuts for breakfast," Mr. Nomad replied.

"Yeah, that's true," Kellan said.

"How long until we reach Isla Mordaz?" Bruce asked.

"Shouldn't be long now. An hour max," Austin said.

After they were done eating, Harper and Bryce helped clean up and put things back the way they were.

"All hands on deck," Captain Dawson shouted, and then he said to Mr. Nomad, "The rains have started again. Make sure we're putting gun powder away and not letting it get wet."

"Aye aye, Captain," Mr. Nomad replied.

The rain began to get heavier as the Black Mist sailed closer and closer to Isla Mordaz.

"I can't get enough of this rain!" Harper said, smiling. "It's so nice."

"I like it, too," Kellan said, looking at her.

"Grab ahold of something. We're going under again," Captain Dawson shouted.

"Aye aye, Captain," the crew shouted back.

This time, Harper decided to tie herself down with Bryce.

"Give me your hand," Bryce said.

When Kellan heard that, his jealousy raged inside. He wanted to be by her side again, with her looking to him for help. He soon regrouped, and he held on to a pole, strapping his ankle to the bottom, as the ship began to sink.

Harper held Bryce's hand and held her breath. The Black Mist sank so fast that she felt like a water hose had sprayed her down with cold, crisp water in December. But the feeling left seconds after the ship resurfaced.

"Why is the water so cold?" Harper asked, trembling.

"Sometimes the artic water washes in. It depends on what's happening on Isla Mordaz. The other ocean water has normal temperatures," Kellan responded. "Can I get you your bag or a blanket?"

"Yes, please! Can you untie us first?" Harper replied.

"Certainly," Kellan said.

After he had untied Harper and Bryce, Kellan went and grabbed Harper's backpack, then reached in and pulled out her sweatshirt. He came back out and handed it to her, saying, "I hope this helps."

"Thank you," Harper replied. "Can you help me off the ship?"

"Yes, Your Highness," Kellan said, helping her down.

"If you insist on calling me anything other than my name, I prefer 'Princess,'" Harper said.

"Very well," Kellan replied.

When the rest of the crew had gotten off the Black Mist, Harper and Kellan wandered off to a tree.

"I do not want it to be awkward between us," Harper said.

"Why do you think it's awkward?" Kellan asked.

"I saw the look you gave me when I chose to partner with Bryce. Don't tell me you're jealous of him. Are you?" Harper asked.

"I was for a split second," Kellan admitted.

"He's my best friend. I don't think I need to explain that further. Can we just start over?" Harper said.

"Okay, fair enough," Kellan said, smiling. "Let's join the group, or they'll think something is up."

The two walked back toward the group, and they all headed toward the rainforest.

"We can spread out this time," Austin said.

"We're not in search of anything other than ring. If we spread out, we'll cover more ground and maybe find it faster" Kendall said. "I'll go with Austin, Mr. Nomad, and Bruce. Harper, you go with Bryce, Kellan, and Barton. Then split up when you reach the rainforest. We will do the same when we reach the Ebony Woodlands. Captain Dawson can watch the ship this time and gather supplies."

The pirates split up just like Kendall said, then headed in two different directions. On their way to the rainforest, Harper spotted black foxes and small white ferrets that had made their homes along the route leading to the rainforest. The trees that towered over them provided shelter for these animals, forming arches around their roots. Fairies also came by on occasion, reshaping them or adding draping leaves to create a more private space for them. Ducks and swans could also be seen in the creeks and streams that ran through the rainforest. When they arrived back at the treehouse, Harper and Bryce decided to go inside, letting Kellan and Barton explore the outside area that surrounded it. Once inside the treehouse, Harper and Bryce walked into the kitchen, only to find two backpacks.

"Look!" Bryce said, pointing to the bags.

"Let's open them and see what's inside," Harper said.

When they had opened the bags, they discovered several items inside, including a flashlight, waters, and two small bows with sharp, metal arrows. They also had crackers, tuna, and berries, all kept cool by a floating ice cloud. The bag contained two knives and two small shields. There was also magic mermaid dust, along with an emerald-green ring that matched the sea-foam color of the dust. Lastly, there was a note. *Please do not harm the creatures you are about to encounter unless absolutely necessary. And use items wisely.*

"What could this mean? We didn't plan to have another long adventure, and even if we had, who will we encounter?" Harper asked.

"Yeah, I agree," Bryce said.

"It's almost as if we have a mission, but where? And how do we know where to go?" Harper said.

"Let's explore outside," Bryce replied as he put the backpack on and handed Harper hers.

Harper put on her backpack, then closed and locked the front door. She stood to the right of the treehouse after climbing down the steps. As she stood there and looked around, she noticed a line of rocks that had formed just outside the willow trees surrounding the treehouse.

"Bryce, look," she said. "There is a curious line dividing us from the right side of the island. This was not here before, was it?"

"Hmm, maybe we should see what's on the other side," Bryce said.

"Good idea. It doesn't look like anything special, but something tells me there is more there than meets the eye," Harper said.

After Harper and Bryce set foot on the land to the other side of the rocks, they walked straight and turned left when they came upon a rock bridge that was built out of the same stones that had formed the line Harper had seem. They walked across the bridge. After they got to the end of that bridge, the scenery changed.

"It sounds like a jungle. And look, the bridge has changed from rocks to wood. The treehouse seems far now," Harper said.

"This place is amazing," Bryce said, staring at a pterodactyl in the sky.

"Wow, I hadn't seen that. Look, Bryce!" Harper said as she came face to face with a triceratops.

Harper pet the dinosaur, and as she walked past it, she saw that there was a herd of iguanodons, stegosauruses, and ankylosauruses nearby, as well. They were both in awe over what they were seeing, and they continued to admire the land several minutes after crossing the bridge.

"Look, there are long-neck dinosaurs, too," Harper said.

"This isn't a jungle. It is a land just for dinosaurs, which explains why the trees seem so tall," Bryce said.

As the two friends walked farther, they saw parasaurolophuses and their babies feeding on the plants and drinking the water from the lake that was located on the far-right side of the land. The farther they got in the land of Jurassic creatures, the more they realized that being there did not exempt them from the dangers that world could present. The island had a volcano on the far-left side, and there were a lot of different breeds of dinosaurs that could potentially pose a threat to them, though they hadn't seen any yet.

"Bryce, why is the ground trembling?" Harper asked.

"Oh no, hide! That is definitely a T-Rex!" Bryce said.

"How do you know? What if it's worse?" Harper said.

"Don't worry. We are well equipped to protect ourselves, but first we hide. Quick, run up that tree," Bryce said.

"Up? No, let's go below, under the arch of the tree. The hanging leaf doors will hide us," Harper said.

The two hid underneath the trees roots and waited while two T-Rex walked past them, hunting for food.

"You know we have tranquilizers in our bags, too, right?" Bryce whispered.

"Shhh, yes, but I think hiding is best right now," Harper replied.

The trembling of the ground began to get farther and farther away, and when it had stopped, Harper and Bryce stepped out from under the arch. They walked into the forest and had just gotten past two other trees when the ground began to tremble again. They looked at each other. Bryce was gripped with fear. Although Harper was afraid of what might be headed toward them, she acted quickly and opened her backpack, took a small bottle of the mermaid pixie dust out, and took out the tranquilizer guns she had (there were two). Harper handed one to Bryce and said, "Get ready to use it. Don't be afraid. You got this!"

Bryce took a deep breath and grabbed the tranquilizer gun just as a huge Spinosaurus spotted them. The dinosaur roared and headed closer to them.

"Why are we waiting around?" Bryce shouted.

The Spinosaurus got closer and closer, and then Harper ran toward it, took out her dust, and shouted, "Petrificus totalus dinosauria."

The dinosaur suddenly froze completely in its tracks, then collapsed on the ground with a loud thud, making the ground tremble. After a few minutes, the dust settled, and Harper and Bryce ran toward the nearest willow tree.

"Let's climb the tree while we figure out where we're going," Harper said.

"What do you mean?" Bryce said, climbing up the willow tree.

"Well, you read that note that was in our bags. We must not harm the creatures we encounter unless absolutely necessary, and right then it wasn't necessary to kill the Spinosaurus."

"You mean..." Oh no!" Bryce said.

"Yes, we're going to have to go back and reverse the spell. We have to plan an escape route," Harper replied.

"Okay, let's start by exploring the rest of the willow trees in this area," Bryce said.

"Okay, let's go. I'm just not sure where we will find this ring," Harper said.

The two friends took off, heading farther into the small field of willow trees, and they came across one that was in the middle. It had purple leaves.

"I've never seen a willow with purple leaves before," Harper said.

"Me either. It's curious," Bryce replied.

This willow tree had dragon fruits growing on it, except at the front of the tree. The fruit was covered by baby ferns that were also purple, and they helped camouflage the fruits' bright-pink color. When Bryce and Harper picked two of the dragon fruits to have as a snack later, the willow tree revealed a door.

"Look, Bryce! Let's go inside!" Harper said.

"Okay," Bryce said, following Harper inside the willow tree.

Inside, they found a bathroom with a shower, a bed to sleep in, and a sink with ice-cold water.

"This is so nice. We have everything we need now in order to escape from the meat-eating dinosaurs," Harper said.

"Yes, until they follow us," Bryce said. "What happens if they destroy our food supplies, or the tree itself?"

"I have a feeling this tree is different from the others. Although it's not exempt from the dangers of this world, it has been given ways to avoid it," Harper said.

"But how do you know? Another feeling?" Bryce asked.

"Yeah, something like that," Harper said.

After the two friends had looked inside the willow tree, Harper wrote down directions so they could remember the location of the tree again. They continued to look around the area, walked past the willow trees and going back into the redwood forest. As Harper and Bryce walked to the center of the forest, they uncovered an odd door attached to one of the trees.

"Why would there be a door attached to this tree?" Bryce asked.

"I don't know. Let's find out," Harper said.

The tree had steps that had been built into it, and Harper used them to climb up into the hollow opening of the tree.

"What are you doing?" Bryce said.

"I want to see where this leads. Are you coming with me?" Harper asked.

Bryce climbed the steps into the tree and closed the tree's door. As soon as the door closed, they were transported back to the willow tree they had previously been inside.

"We discovered a passageway!" Bryce said as he sat on the bed inside the willow tree.

"Yes, and you know what that means," Harper said.

"Oh no, we have to go back and reverse the spell that we cast on that dinosaur, don't we?" Bryce replied.

"Yes, come on," Harper said, heading out of the willow tree.

Bryce closed the door behind him and followed Harper back to where the Spinosaurus was.

"Where is he?" Harper asked.

"Are you sure this is the right spot?" Bryce replied.

"Yes! The spell must have worn off. I bet it only lasted long enough for us to get away," Harper replied.

"Well, let's go before it comes back and we have to cast another spell," Bryce said.

The two friends walked back into the forest, going to the area where they had found the passageway, and continued to walk past it. When they came across a creek, they stopped to have a snack. Harper took two dragon fruits out of her bag, along with golden cheese crackers and two water bottles.

"Hey, look at these knives," Bryce said.

"Let's look at them after we eat," Harper said. "Okay, do you prefer cheese crackers or pretzel sticks?"

"Pretzel sticks, please," Bryce replied.

"Okay, here you go," Harper said, handing Bryce his food.

"The creek has small fish in it, and baby lizards that look like mini dinosaurs," Bryce said.

"I noticed that, too. I wonder where it leads," Harper said.

"What makes you think it leads anywhere?" Bryce replied.

"Well, I'm assuming it does. After all, the water can't just run nonstop, and even if it did, it would still go somewhere."

"Ugh, fine. We'll follow it," Bryce said.

After the two friends had finished eating, Bryce took the knives out and gave one to Harper, asking, "What do you think these are for?"

"I'm not sure, but I think we will find out if are in danger again," Harper said, and then she hit the button on the knife. "Woah, mine turns into a glam station. Makeup, clothes. Everything I need is all here."

"Mine creates a hole in the ground," Bryce said.

"What?" Harper asked, turning to look at the hole. "That's not a hole. It's a portal. Close it."

Bryce hit the button on his knife, and the portal disappeared.

"Okay, it's gone," he said, looking at Harper.

"Okay, let's put these away," Harper said.

They continued walking, following the creek until they reached a small lake and an open field of grass that was surrounded by tall pine trees.

"Oh my God! What is that?" Bryce said, freezing in his tracks.

"Are you going to be afraid of everything we encounter? He's gorgeous!" Harper said, smiling.

"Don't get so close. We don't know how dangerous that thing is," Bryce replied.

"He doesn't look dangerous," Harper said.

Harper walked closer to the gryphon that was lying in the middle of the green field, reaching out her hand. The gryphon was half eagle, half lion. It was blue and gray, and it had a yellow beak and yellow feet. When the gryphon realized he was not alone, he got up and approached Harper's hand. He sniffed her hand, and she stood still until she felt is was safe to pet him.

Harper softly stroked the back of the gryphon's head, and the creature stood still, enjoying Harper's company. After Bryce saw this, he got closer and tried the same thing. Once they were all acquainted with each other, Harper and Bryce were able to spend time feeding it and exploring the gryphon's home, which was located inside a brown cave on the other side of the pine trees.

"Something is different here. I think we have entered a different world now, and it appears to separate the dinosaurs from the gryphons," Harper said to Bryce.

"How would you know that? Oh wait, another feeling?" Bryce asked.

"Well, have you seen any dinosaurs since the creek?" Harper asked.

"No, good point. They seemed to get smaller or become reptiles after the creek," Bryce replied.

"Do we have other resources inside the backpack? The sun is beginning to set, and I want more time with our friend," Harper said.

"Let me look," Bryce said as he searched in his backpack. "We have a blanket, a pillow, and an inflatable bed."

"Okay, let's set up camp in the gryphon's cave. What should we name him?" Harper said.

"Hmm, how about Hendrix?" Bryce replied.

"I really do like that. Hendrix it is," Harper said.

The two friends set up their sleeping arrangements and went into the cave for the night. Harper used two sticks to create a fire and, shortly after, fell asleep on her mattress. Bryce waited a while before putting out the fire, but once Hendrix was asleep, he put the fire out and went to sleep.

***

The next morning, Hendrix went to search for food. Meanwhile, Harper was up and was getting ready for the day inside the cave, and Bryce was sleeping in. After Harper was done, she put everything back into her backpack and reached in to see what she could find for food. At the bottom of her backpack, she found four eggs, so she went outside to start a fire and cook them. She grabbed a pan from inside her backpack, scooped up some water from the lake, and set the pan on the fire, putting the eggs inside so they could boil. When the eggs were done, she took them out of the pan, let the pan cool on a rock, and put the eggs in a cup. She peeled two of the eggs and ate them, leaving the other two for Bryce. She buried the egg peels in the ground and packed up the pan once it had cooled.

When Harper went back inside the cave to see if Bryce had woken up yet, she saw that he was still asleep, so she put the eggs down beside him, left a note by his bed, and headed out to continue exploring the area. As she walked across the green field, she spotted a yellow flower. The flower glistened and sparkled with what seemed to be gold pixie dust or glitter. The flower drew her in, and she begin to walk in its direction, not paying attention to who was near or where she was going. When she finally reached the flower, she bent down and snapped it with the knife from her bag, then placed it in a plastic bag. She knew that if Kendall placed a spell on it, it could a while. When she was done putting the flower in her backpack, she looked up and saw nests. The nests had eggs in them, and they were in close proximity to each other.

Oh no, these are dinosaur eggs, Harper thought to herself.

Just then, she spotted a velociraptor. Once she had made eye contact, the dinosaur began to caw and call for help, and three other raptors appeared in a matter of minutes. Frozen with fear, she began to think. *If I run, they'll chase me. If I hide, they'll dig into the spot. What can I do to stop them?* She quickly reached into her backpack as the raptors got closer and closer to her, and she pulled out the mermaid dust. This time, the dust was blue, and she realized it would continue to change depending on the danger she was facing. She opened the small jar, took the dust, and threw it at the raptors. The dust momentarily confused them, and she then quickly cast a spell to petrify all of the raptors. As soon as they became momentarily frozen, she began to run as fast as she could, heading back toward the gryphon's home. Once she had gone past the flowers, she knew she was safe, and she stopped to catch her breath and drink some water.

"There you are! Thanks for the eggs. I'm all packed up and ready to continue to explore. I was worried something might have happened to you," Bryce said, approaching Harper.

"I decided to explore the other side of that flower, and it wasn't a good idea. I ran into raptors," Harper said.

"Raptors? I thought they were gone now," Bryce replied.

"Yes, they are while we're here with Hendrix, but not in that part of this world," Harper said.

"I think we should take Hendrix," Bryce said.

"What do you mean?" Harper asked.

"Let's ride him. He can fly, and we can see what areas we want to avoid," Bryce said.

"Great idea. Where is he?" Harper asked.

"Follow me. He's by the lake," Bryce said.

The two friends climbed on Hendrix's back and held on tight as he soared over the land of dinosaurs. As he was passing over the forests and mountains, Harper spotted orange and yellow trees.

"Hendrix, lower us down," Harper said.

"What? We're not going to land," Bryce said.

"Yes, we are! Look, it's the crew!" Harper said.

"How did they get here?" Bryce asked.

"They must have gotten worried," Harper replied.

When Hendrix had landed, Harper walked over to the crew and asked, "What are you all doing here?"

"We got worried when you didn't return. Kellan arranged a search, and we ended up here in this forest. We haven't been able to find a way out," Kendall said.

"There was a hidden passageway near the willow trees back at the treehouse, and it led us here," Kellan said.

"Let's get back to the treehouse and regroup," Austin said.

"Okay, but first we have to drop Hendrix off at his cave," Bryce replied.

"Everyone, hop on and hold on," Harper said.

Hendrix spread his wings and took off, soaring in the sky, the cool, windy breeze blowing in their faces. They were happy to be together again. When Hendrix landed, the pirates agreed to stay the night.

"We can explore the lake. Are you down for a swim?" Harper asked Kellan.

"Yeah, let's do it," Kellan said.

Harper and Kellan both jumped into the lake and began to swim and explore the world underneath the lake. As they swam around, Harper spotted a small treasure chest and dug it out with a rock. When she swam back to shore, she took off her swimming gear.

"Kellan, look!" Harper said.

Kellan walked over to her and helped her get the chest open. Inside, there was a card that had *Beware. The jewel before you holds power beyond this land. Guard it, for you have been chosen to be the keeper. In the wrong hands, it will cause major destruction!* written on it After reading the card aloud, Harper twisted the handle on the box, and the door inside opened, revealing a ring.

"It's the rin—" Harper was about to shout, but Kellan grabbed her and placed his hand over her mouth.

"Shhh, we don't know who else is out here in this part of the forest," Kellan said.

"Ugh, sorry, but can you believe we found it! The green one we found must have been a decoy to trick others," Harper replied.

"Yes, you're smart! For now, I think it's best if only you and I know about the ring. It'll be our secret," Kellan said, smiling.

"Deal," Harper said, grinning.

"Make sure you take it back to the treehouse, and whatever you do, make sure it's in a secure place. I'll help you by stalling the others. You can put it in your backpack for now," Kellan said.

"Okay, it's a plan," Harper said.

Harper put the ring in her backpack and asked Kellan to watch it as she jumped back into the lake.

"Hey, Bryce," Kellan shouted.

"What's up?" Bryce replied.

"Watch Harper's bag! I'm diving in," Kellan said.

"Okay, I've got it," Bryce said, putting it on his back.

Kellan swam after Harper, curious to see what else she would discover.

Harper felt something poke her leg, and when she looked down, she spotted a feather that was different colors. She grabbed the feather and swam back up to shore, Kellan following.

"What did you find?" he asked.

"It's a feather. It looks like a peacock's feather, but it has colors that are different from what I'm used to seeing or reading about," Harper replied.

"Peacocks are good luck. They mean protection and beauty," Kellan said.

Harper looked up as Kellan said that and saw two peacocks in the distance. One of them was white, and the other was lavender.

"The sun is reflecting something off of them. They have something we need. I'm following them," Harper said.

"Wait, your bag, and we should have Bryce come with us," Kellan replied.

"Okay. Bryce! My bag. Hurry over," Harper shouted.

"Coming!" Bryce replied. He ran over to where Harper and Kellan were and handed Harper her bag, then asked, "What's up? Where are we headed now?"

"We're following those two peacocks. Harper thinks they have something we need. Check your backpack. How many portals do you have?" Kellan asked.

Bryce looked in his backpack and found two portals, then said, "I only have two. Wait, why?"

"Okay, give one to the pirates. They'll need to get back to the ship and head out to sea soon. The portal will know where they need to go," Kellan said.

Bryce ran back over to the pirates and explained what Kellan had said. It seemed like the peacocks were waiting patiently for Harper to start heading their way.

"Harper, I took the liberty of grabbing your invisibility coats before I left the treehouse. You accidently forget them there after you tried them on," Kellan said.

"Thank you!" Harper replied.

"Use them to get back to the treehouse safely. I'm going to go in an hour and rent out a boat for us. That way, we can find our way back to Sterling Krystalline. So, I'll need the other portal," Kellan said.

Harper took the robes and stuck them inside her backpack. After a flash of blue light, the pirates were gone, and Bryce ran back to where Kellan and Harper were after saying goodbye to Hendrix. The three of them headed toward the peacocks. By that time, the birds had started walking away, and the three friends ran to catch up to them. The peacocks led Harper, Bryce, and Kellan to a cave mountain that was lit up by yellow salt rocks. They walked deeper into the cave, unsure of where they were headed, only to find baby peacocks.

"Oh my goodness! They are so cute! They are a family!" Harper exclaimed.

As she got closer, she noticed the white peacock sitting on an object.

"Is that an egg?" Bryce asked.

"No, it's not. It's okay, fellow. I'm just going to remove you gently," Kellan said to the bird as he grabbed the crystal ball underneath it.

"A crystal ball? There must be a reason we found this. We have not heard from Corbin in a while. I am sure he didn't just disappear," Harper said.

"Well, you better quickly ask it about his whereabouts. I hear something coming," Bryce said.

Harper grabbed the crystal ball from Kellan and asked it to show her Corbin. The crystal ball revealed that Corbin was asking another crystal ball about their whereabouts, and he had just entered the land of dinosaurs on a brown-horned dragon.

"There are only two of these crystal balls, and now you each have one, but that also means he's closer to us than we thought. We have to get back now," Kellan said.

"Guys, remember when I said I heard something coming? Look!" Bryce said, pointing to the entrance of the cave.

"What is that?" Kellan asked.

"Let's go find out!" Harper said.

The three friends walked outside, taking the crystal ball with them.

"It's a dragon," Harper said.

"Let's ride it back to the entrance," Bryce said.

"Crystal ball, show us Corbin," Kellan said, climbing onto the dragon.

The dragon lived with the peacocks and served as their protector. It was large and yellow in color, though there were some green specks on its body.

Once all three friends were on the back of the dragon, it took off into the sky, heading toward the entrance of the dinosaur forest. The crystal ball showed Corbin in the middle of the same forest, and Kellan was prepared to hide Bryce and Harper from his sight, but when the yellow dragon landed, Corbin was nowhere to be found.

"We have to move quickly," Kellan said as they all waved goodbye to the yellow dragon.

Two seconds after the dragon had flown away, Kellan spotted Corbin, but before he could see them, the three friends had disappeared onto the bridge that led back to the treehouse.

"That was a close call," Kellan said.

"Yeah, I think Corbin knows the ring we're looking for is in this land. The crystal ball revealed its location to him," Harper said.

"He may know the location, but he doesn't know the color or details of it," Kellan replied.

"Neither do we, so how will we find it?" Bryce asked.

"Bryce, you can't tell a soul, but we found it," Harper said.

"You what?" Bryce replied.

"In the lake. It's orange," Harper said.

"Wow, okay," Bryce said.

"We have to put it in a safe inside the treehouse," Harper said.

The three friends crossed the line of rocks and found themselves back at the treehouse.

"You go inside, rest up, and hide that ring. I am going to go get us a boat, and I'll be back. Bryce, I need your portal now," Kellan said.

Bryce handed Kellan the portal, and he and Harper went up the treehouse stairs so they could put the ring away. Once they had found a spot where they could hide the ring, they both cleaned up and then went to bed.

Chapter Six

Isle of the Ikkakkujuu

Meanwhile, back at sea, the pirates had stopped on a foreign island called Isle of the Ikkakkujuu. It had gained the name because it was in the shape of a unicorn skull.

"Did you see this the last time we were near Isla Mordaz?" Austin asked Bruce and Barton.

"No, we were thinking the same thing," Barton replied.

"It must have been hidden, or we missed it in the rain," Mr. Nomad said.

"Why are we here?" Kendall asked.

"We need to restock on food, especially shrimp or fish, since we are pretty far from land right now," Mr. Nomad replied.

"We'll be an hour tops. Feel free to explore," Captain Dawson said.

The pirates got down from the Black Mist and went inside the unicorn skull to see what they could find. Kendall spotted several rocks within the gigantic rock they were inside of. Shortly after, mermaids shortly swam up to the shore and sat on those rocks.

"Are you all from here?" Kendall asked.

"That depends. If you're referring to Isle of the Ikkakkujuu, which is where we are, then yes. We like to watch the sunset from this location. My name is Pyra, and these are my sisters," a mermaid said.

"Isle of the what?" Kendall asked.

"The word is Ikkakkujuu. It is Japanese for unicorn. Back when the island was first discovered, the pirates who landed here were from Japan, and they decided on a name in their native language. Since it was fitting, it has stayed that way ever since. There are different kinds of unicorns and other rare animals on the island. If you're planning on staying for a while, you may encounter them, at least if you are brave enough to fight the dangers and uncover legends of the island," Pyra said.

"Every island has a legend, but dangers? What kind of dangers?" Austin asked.

"Quicksand, spiders, and wolves can also be found on the island," Pyra replied.

"Spiders? Those aren't scary!" Bruce said.

"That depends on your perception of them," Pyra said.

"Hey, girls, another lovely sunset tonight, isn't it?" Kelsey asked.

"Kelsey?" Kendall said.

"Do I know you?" Kelsey replied.

"No, but I know you. We're friends with Harper, your cousin," Kendall said.

"Funny, she's never mentioned you. I'm friends with Pyra and her sisters," Kelsey said.

"How exactly do you two know each other?" Austin asked.

"Why don't you all take a seat? I'll explain how we met," Kelsey said.

Kelsey used a nail and a rock to stab the rope attached to her small boat into the sand on the shore. She sat down and watched the pirates take a seat a few feet away from her. The sun was setting as she began to tell the story, starting with her journey to the island.

***

Kelsey was sitting on sand that was not far from her and Spencer's beach house.

"I love this beautiful weather. Don't you, Spencer?" she asked.

"Oh yes, it's perfect. I am glad we are on vacation for a while. I needed some time to get away from my busy routine," Spencer said.

After watching the sun set, the girls drank some tea before bed, and when the sun rose the next morning, they changed into their bathing suits and headed out for a swim in the ocean. The girls felt the water with their toes first, then slowly began to walk farther into the water, not stopping until their legs were fully submerged. The girls got used to the temperature of the water and began to swim west.

"Hey, Spencer, come over here. You have got to see this," Kelsey said, letting the waves carry her to shore once again.

"I'm coming. What's the rush?" Spencer replied.

"Look," Kelsey said, pointing to the Isle of the Ikkakkujuu.

"Oh my word, it's a unicorn skull, and it's gorgeous! Did you know this was here?" Spencer asked.

"No, I didn't. I just decided to swim west instead of east this time, and before I could continue swimming farther out, I accidently hit my knee against what seemed to be a huge rock," Kelsey said.

"Are you okay? If you're up for it, let's explore the island," Spencer said.

"Yes, I'll be okay. I'll ice my knee when we get back to the beach house," Kelsey replied.

As they began to walk, Kelsey's knee began to slowly turn purple, but she brushed it off and decided to rest her knee when she was back in her room later. The island the girls were on had tide pools with baby star fish, coral, and clams.

"Where should we explore first?" Kelsey asked.

"Let's see what's over here by these rocks. It looks like stepping-stones," Spencer said as she stepped onto the first rock.

"Let's swim underneath and see if we can find any crabs for dinner tonight," Kelsey said, following her.

"Okay, that sounds good," Spencer said.

The girls jumped into the ocean, and when they were beneath the water, they opened their eyes, only to discover an underwater cave that was almost as big as a one-story house. Since the girls had swum down from the steppingstones, they were already in the middle of the cave, and they could see seaweed drapes from both side entrances. They appeared to hide the cave's location, along with different-colored coral and rocks that formed the legs and hooved feet of the unicorn cave, which seemed to be stuck in the sand. Half of its body was on the shore, and the other half was underneath, almost as if the rocks had been purposefully shaped that way. Before the girls could swim deeper into the cave, they had to swim back up to the surface.

"I almost ran out of breath," Spencer said, breathing heavily.

"Me, too. We need to find something we can use to finish exploring that cave, even if it means learning to hold our breath longer," Kelsey said.

"Let's go look on the island. Maybe we will find what we need in order to be able to dive deeper into the ocean," Spencer said.

The girls set off to the middle of the island, which looked like it could be the body of a unicorn from a distance, and began to look for shops that had swimming gear. After walking for over an hour, the girls stopped for a break.

"I'm tired now. Do we have water in your backpack?" Spencer asked.

"Yes, here's the last of it," Kelsey said, handing Spencer her water bottle.

Above them, two phoenixes appeared and were sitting quietly in their nest, which was in the center of a large redwood tree. The birds were fierce-looking and had black beaks and feet. A majestic purple-and-blue color covered their entire bodies from head to legs. The phoenixes watched the girls below them.

Meanwhile, a pack of wolves had also crept into the girls' space, and the louder they spoke, the closer they got.

"Do you hear that?" Spencer said.

"Hear what?" Kelsey asked.

"Shhh, we're not alone anymore," Spencer said as she looked around.

"AHH!!!" Kelsey screamed as a wolf jumped out of the bushes.

The animal stared at her and began to growl loudly, and its wolf pack followed and came to the center of the island, surrounding them.

"What are we going to do? We're surrounded!" Spencer shouted.

"Just stay behind me," Kelsey said.

Before the wolves could attack, the birds that had been sitting in the tree flew down in front of the wolves, and as they put their wings together, they emitted a flash of light from their eyes. The light created a protective circle around the girls and blinded the wolves, forcing them to retreat. The wolves ran in the opposite direction they had come from, and the girls were relived they had been saved.

"Thank you!" Spencer shouted as she waved to the phoenixes, which flew back up to their home in the redwood tree.

"That was such a close call. I think we should turn around and head back now," Kelsey said.

"Good idea," Spencer replied.

The girls started back toward the shore of the island, and as they walked, they began to hear footsteps, almost like someone else had joined them or was following them.

"Please don't tell me the wolves are back," Kelsey said.

"Oh no, I thought I was the only one hearing things," Spencer said.

Despite the footsteps, the girls continued to walk until they reached a meadow that had a waterfall and a flower garden full of pink lotuses, red and yellow marigolds, orange dwarf water lilies, and lavender plants.

"Did we come through this garden on our way in?" Kelsey asked.

"No, I definitely would have remembered. We should refill our water bottles," Spencer said. Before she could fill her bottle to the top, she spotted a unicorn and said, "Kelsey, come quick! Look!"

The unicorn looked at the girls but continued to walk toward the flowers. It stopped at a water lily and ate it.

"It's beautiful," Kelsey said, and they watched it graze among the flowers in the garden.

The girls inched their way closer and closer, until Kelsey could almost touch it with her arm stretched out.

"It's okay. We're not going to hurt you," Spencer said as she stretched out her hand for the unicorn to sniff.

The unicorn did not move or bother to sniff Spencer's hand. It seemed to only be interested in the flowers it was eating.

"Look at its horn. It's glowing," Kelsey said.

"It is glowing. I wonder why," Spencer said, looking closer as she began to pet the creature.

As Spencer continued to pet it, the unicorn bowed down, and magic dust started to pour from its horn. The dust landed on the ground, filling three small jars that had suddenly appeared. When the unicorn was done filling them, the jars glowed until they all had chains they could be picked up by.

"I think these are meant for us to use," Kelsey said, picking them up.

The unicorn then walked over to the waterfall and drank.

"Since there are only three, I'll keep two, and you can wear one," Kelsey said to Spencer.

When the unicorn had finished drinking water, it walked away, going back in the direction it had come from.

"I think we should try this dust when we go back into the water. Maybe we'll be able to see what's beneath the cave portion of this island," Kelsey said.

As more unicorns began to walk into the garden, the girls headed back in the direction they had come from, searching for the shore. After another forty minutes of walking, they found themselves back at the shore.

"Okay, who's going first?" Spencer said.

"I'll do it," Kelsey replied.

Kelsey took one of the small jars around her neck, opened it, and sprinkled some dust into the palm of her hand. She walked over to where the water met the shore, sat down with her legs together, and sprinkled the dust. The dust began to form a dark cloud over her legs, and shortly after she had turned into a blue-and-green lake mermaid. She jumped into the ocean.

Spencer had been watching her, and she followed in her steps, sprinkling dust onto her legs, as well. She turned into a lake mermaid, as well, but her colors were bright pink and orange. After she had jumped into the ocean, she met up with Kelsey underneath the steppingstones.

"Have you seen us? We look like actual lake mermaids, and I can breathe underwater!" Spencer exclaimed.

"Now we can go see what's inside this cave. Come on," Kelsey said, swimming into the cave.

Inside the cave were two treasure chests. One was filled with Caribbean rum, and the other was filled with treasure.

"I wonder who was here before us. There is no way the rum has been here for a long time. It looks new and is still sealed, but why would they leave rum lying about?" Spencer asked

"I'm not sure. Let's go in farther," Kelsey replied.

The girls swam until they came upon another opening inside the cave. This one had seaweed draping down it, and sea leaves served as a door.

"Let's go through it," Kelsey said.

"Right behind you," Spencer replied.

On the other side, there were nine stone seats that had seashells carved into them, and there was a set of mirrors on the cave's walls.

"Wow, these are some cute vanities," Spencer said.

"I agree, but who would use a vanity under the sea?" Kelsey replied.

"We would!" said a voice.

"I can't believe my eyes! Mermaids!" Spencer exclaimed.

"Wow, they're gorgeous. There are so many of them," Kelsey said.

"Nine, to be exact," said the voice again.

The mermaids were different from each other. They were all different colors, and they had different names and personalities. In the middle of the cave space, there were coral seats that attached to the ground. The mermaids all sat in the seats, and Kelsey and Spencer swam closer to them, sitting across from them on two boulders.

"I'm Pyra, and these girls are my sisters. I will introduce you," Pyra said.

Pyra was the oldest mermaid, and she cared for her sisters like a mother would her own children. Her parents had both been killed by pirates after she had turned twelve, leaving her an orphan. She had a red-orange tail, red-orange hair, and black seashells. She wore red-orange eye makeup, and she had long lashes. Gold glitter was on her upper cheeks and on her nose bone. She also had seashells in her hair, which were being used as a hairband. Her lips had a light-golden gloss on them. She was known for her bravery and courage among fellow merfolk.

Her sister Leah, who was two years younger than her, was known for her athletic abilities, and she had brown hair, white seashells, and a white tail. She wore face makeup in various shades of white and brown. She also had long lashes, and she had freckles all along her cheeks. Her lips had a light-pink gloss on them.

Sierra was two years younger than Leah and was known for her kind and gentle spirit toward others. She wore a starfish in her hair to clip up the left portion. She had a yellow tail, jet-black hair, and navy-blue seashells. She also wore face makeup and yellow shadow. She had long lashes, and she also had a beauty spot on the right side of her face. Her lip gloss was light blue, and it sparkled. She had a headband made from coral.

Violet was two years younger than Sierra and was known for her singing abilities. She had a blue tail, blond hair, and silver seashells. She wore blue eye shadow and had long lashes. She wore light-orange lip gloss, and her cheeks were covered with silver glitter. It sparkled, just like Pyra's. She wore a simple, coral headband that had one small starfish attached, and she kept her hair in a braid.

Nova was two years younger than Violet and was known for her gentleness and friendly spirit. She had a purple tail, black hair, and mint seashells. She wore purple eye shadow, had long lashes, and wore a light-purple lip gloss. She kept mint-colored seaweed in her hair and kept it up in a ponytail. She also had dimples when she smiled.

Zoe was two years younger than Nova and was known for her loyalty and cooking skills. She had a pink tail, light-brown hair, and black seashells She wore pink eye shadow and had long lashes. She also wore pink, sparkling glitter on her face, like Pyra and Violet. Her lip gloss was a light shade of black. She wore two starfish in her hair, and they kept both sides of her hair swept back.

Stella was two years younger than Zoe and was known for being a joker and having a great sense of humor. She had a gray tail, orange hair, and pink seashells. She wore gray eye shadow and had long lashes. She also wore light-pink lip gloss. She kept a sea flower in her hair. She switched out the style and color depending on what she found on her adventures.

Hilda was two years younger than Stella and was known for her independence. She had an aquamarine tail, black hair with blue highlights, and yellow seashells. She wore different seashells in her hair, using them as clips, and she wore light-blue eye shadow. She had long lashes. She wore a yellow glitter on her face, like Pyra, Sierra, and Nova.

Hazel was two years younger than Hilda, and at twenty-two she was the youngest mermaid. She was known for her headstrong personality, and she had a bright-orange tail, brown hair, and forest-green seashells. She wore bright-orange eye shadow and had long lashes. She wore green glitter, like Pyra, Sierra, Nova, and Hilda. She wore a forest-green band in her hair. It was made from coral and was covered with black glitter. She often enjoyed watching pirate ships come onto the island. She liked trading things she found at the bottom of the ocean.

When Pyra had finished introducing her sisters to Kelsey and Spencer, Kelsey explained who they were and why they were visiting them.

"Interesting. So, you're both not really lake mermaids, then?" Pyra asked Kelsey.

"That's correct. We were given magic by the unicorns on this island," Spencer replied.

"I have heard a rumor that those mermaids are a lot meaner than we are," Pyra said.

"Me, too, but maybe it's just their appearance. You can't always judge a book by its cover. After all, you're both nice," Hilda said.

"Do you any of you know why there is rum at the entrance of the cave?" Spencer asked.

"Rum?" Pyra said, frowning.

"I do. Don't be mad, Pyra. The last time I went out on one of my adventures, pirates stopped on the island, and I may have had an encounter with one of them. He gave me the rum and asked if I could keep it safe for him," Hazel said.

"You what?" Sierra said angrily.

"I can't believe this! Hazel, you could have been killed or seen by other humans. Contact with humans outside of the ocean is forbidden," Violet said.

"I know. I'm sorry. I was just really curious. I used magic to turn human. My identity was never compromised. I have more of it from the unicorns, and I have a chest full of it here now," Hazel said.

"What I want to know is how you got any in the first place!" Pyra said.

"I found it on the shore when I was exploring. I went out on the sand for a few minutes and found the unicorn magic in a glass container. It was small, and it caught my eye, as the sun was reflecting off of it," Hazel said.

"You must be more careful. Please do not repeat those actions," Pyra said.

"I can't promise that," Hazel said.

"Oh? And why not?" Sierra asked.

"I've met someone," Hazel replied.

"A boy?" Nova asked.

"Yes, he's a pirate," Hazel replied.

"You will not be seeing him again! I can't let you risk it. What happens if he finds out you're a mermaid?" Nova asked.

"We just won't let that happen, will we?" Hazel replied, swimming off toward the rum.

"I'm sorry. I didn't mean to cause so much trouble," Kelsey said.

"It's all right. I'll deal with her later," Pyra replied.

As Kelsey continued to make conversation with the mermaids, Spencer slipped away and went to explore a different section of the cave. She swam past a large space full of lavender kelp and giant clams. It appeared to be where the mermaids slept. Then she came across another space inside the cave, and it was full of giant, feathered blue starfish. While she was admiring the beauty of these creatures, a dolphin swam past her as it chased a group of orange-and-red-freckled jellyfish. As soon as she saw this, Spencer swam back the way she had come so she could find Kelsey.

"Kelsey, come quick! There's a dolphin. Follow me, and I'll show you," Spencer exclaimed.

"Right behind you, Spence!" Kelsey said. "It was so nice meeting all of you. We'll be back soon to visit again."

"Have fun with the dolphins," Pyra shouted as she waved.

Once the girls had said goodbye to the mermaids, they swam into the forest of feathered blue starfish and paused in the middle as they looked for the dolphin.

"Woah! This place is amazing!" Kelsey said.

After a few minutes, the dolphin swam past them, chasing the jellyfish, just like it had done before.

"Oh my! He's gorgeous!" Kelsey exclaimed.

"I wonder if he has a family," Spencer said.

The girls continued deeper into the ocean forest and spotted dolphins of a different color nearby.

"That must be them!" Spencer said.

"No way. They're different colors," Kelsey replied.

"Maybe the dolphin we saw is just the odd ball, at least color-wise. He must have markings that identify him to his family," Spencer said.

"Maybe. We better get going. We can't let the sun go down before we swim back. Let's hunt for crabs and go back to shore," Kelsey said.

"No need. I found some in the starfish forest earlier, and they're in my backpack. I sprinkled dust on them, and they stopped moving," Spencer said.

"Okay, let's head home, then," Kelsey said, *and the girls started back toward the mermaid cave, then began to swim up higher, searching for land.*

While they were on their way back to shore, going up sea levels, two hammerhead sharks began swimming in the same direction.

"Shark!" Spencer shouted, *increasing her speed.*

Kelsey increased her speed and tried to catch up to Spencer, but she could not because the injury on her knee had gotten worse since she had been swimming for over an hour. Before she could make it to shore, one of the sharks attempted to bite her. It failed, getting caught in a huge net. Frightened by what could have happened, Kelsey fainted and began to sink to the bottom of the ocean.

Pyra and her sisters had been hiding from the sharks and had seen what happened, so they rushed over to her, grabbed her arm, and began to swim toward the shore.

"We must not be seen," Pyra shouted.

"Hazel, do you have your magic?" Nova asked.

"Yes, I have it. I'll get out of the water with her and return after I make sure she is okay," Hazel said.

When they reached the shore, the mermaids helped push Kelsey closer to the sand. Once Kelsey and Hazel were both out of the water, Hazel pushed on Kelsey's stomach to make sure any water she may have swallowed got out. After two attempts, Kelsey spat up the water and began to breathe again.

"Oh, thank goodness. You scared me there, and I wasn't sure what I was going to do. Are you okay?" Hazel said.

"I am now. Thank you for coming to my rescue. Where's Spencer?" Kelsey replied.

Hazel looked around and saw Spencer in the distance. She was hiding behind a rock, as a pirate ship had pulled up to the island. The ship was orange and aqua, and Hazel knew the Autumn Corpse crew had returned.

"Spencer!" Hazel shouted, waving her hands.

When Spencer saw her with Kelsey, she ran over to them and said, "Thank God! I was worried about her. What happened?"

"My knee is getting worse. It hurts really bad, and it is getter more and more purple," Kelsey replied.

"Can you walk?" Spencer asked.

"Yes, I think I can," Kelsey replied.

"Okay, we will deal with it when we get back to the beach house. We have to go. Pirates have arrived on the island," Spencer said to Kelsey, helping her up.

"I'll distract them. My friend is on that ship," Hazel said.

"The guy you have been seeing?" Spencer asked, grinning.

"Yes, his name is Blaze. I can introduce you quickly. Follow me," Hazel said.

The girls walked over to the ship, and Hazel waited until she saw Blaze, then said, "Hey, stranger."

"Hey, I was hoping I would run into you. This is my friend and mate Keaton Stone. Who do you have with you?" Blaze asked.

"These are my friends Kelsey and Spencer," Hazel said.

"It is so nice to meet you, ladies," Keaton said, smiling.

"Likewise. We are actually on our way home, but we will be back to visit," Kelsey said.

"We could give you a lift and stop by your place before we leave. We actually stopped to grab some food. Our kitchen was a bit empty. We should be loading and leaving soon," Keaton said.

"Keaton and Blaze! Let's go!" Captain Hamish said.

"See? Fast enough? Are you coming?" Keaton said to Spencer, holding out his hand.

Spencer smiled, grabbed his hand, and walked aboard the Autumn Corpse. Kelsey followed her, and they waved goodbye to Hazel.

"I'll be back again. Keep my necklace with you as a promise of my return," Blaze said, staring into Hazel's eyes.

Blaze pulled Hazel closer to himself and kissed her passionately before leaving. When the Autumn Corpse had left the dock, Hazel began to walk toward the ocean. When she reached the water, she made sure no one else was watching before sprinkling the dust on her legs. She turned back into a mermaid and swam back toward the lagoon to report back to Pyra and her sisters.

Meanwhile, Kelsey and Spencer got to know Blaze and Keaton better while they were aboard their ship, and when Kelsey and Spencer got home, they talked about their short voyage on the Autumn Corpse while Kelsey iced her knee. The swelling on her knee had gotten worse since the last time she had checked it.

"How's your knee feeling?" Spencer asked.

"It looks worse than it feels," Kelsey said. "What do you think about Keaton?"

"He's super sweet, and his eyes are so dreamy," Spencer replied, blushing.

"So, you like him?" Kelsey asked.

"I mean, maybe, but who knows if he even likes me that way. For now, I'm just glad we're friends," Spencer said.

"Well, don't worry. We'll be seeing them again soon," Kelsey said.

"Can't wait, but for now I better get to bed. I have to be at work tomorrow, and I can't be late," Spencer said.

Both girls said goodnight and went to bed.

***

"That's how we know each other," Kelsey said after she finished telling her story.

"So, you're friends with the Autumn Corpse crew? They are our rivals. That is not going to sit well with Harper, although Kellan is friends with Blaze," Austin said.

"Maybe what you need is time to get to know the crew aboard the Autumn Corpse. They may become your allies," Pyra said.

"So, does this story have anything to do with the legends you mentioned?" Barton asked.

"Well, one legend says that a blue necklace with a large gem was left behind on this island by a former pirate. The pirates believed the necklace had magic powers, but they were unable to unleash those powers because the necklace was dropped in a cave. The location is apparently directly underneath us, but we have not seen such a necklace on the island or underneath it. Another rumor suggests that mermaids did find it long ago, and they hid it away from the world, putting it somewhere where travelers could not find it. It remains there to this day. Is that an item Harper is searching for?" Pyra asked.

"No, it isn't at the moment, but this has been very informative. Thank you, Pyra," Kendall said.

"It was nice meeting you all. I'm afraid we must be going now," Austin said.

"Don't be strangers. Come back again soon," Pyra replied as she, the other mermaids, and Kelsey waved goodbye.

The pirates then got back on the Black Mist and took off in the open ocean once again.

Chapter Seven

Revisiting Familiar Places

Back at the treehouse, Harper and Bryce had awoken to a rainy day, and as they watched the rain fall, they wondered when Kellan would return.

"I hope he was able to get a ship back onto this island, even if it's small," Harper said.

"Me, too. The rain is picking up," Bryce replied.

After having some tea and crackers, they packed up their belongings and locked the treehouse doors.

"Are you sure this is a good idea?" Bryce asked.

"Yes, Kellan doesn't have a way of getting directly back to the treehouse. If we walk toward him, it will be easier for him," Harper responded.

The two friends began to walk toward the lake at the center of the island, where they had decided to wait for Kellan. When they arrived there, the rain had stopped, but the weather was still gloomy.

"Did you bring water in your backpack?" Bryce asked.

"Yes," Harper replied, handing Bryce a water bottle.

As they were drinking their water, Kellan arrived with Blaze. Kellan had disguised himself to look like a commoner, and less like a pirate, after he had seen Blaze on Python Cove. He was hoping to gain the trust of his friend and his friend's crew so he could ride on their ship and go back to Isla Mordaz.

"What are you two doing here? I thought we agreed to meet back up on a different part of the island?"

"We figured it would be easier to just wait here," Bryce replied.

"Who's your friend?" Harper asked.

"This is Blaze. He's part of the crew on the Autumn Corpse," Kellan replied.

"Isn't that an enemy ship?" Bryce whispered.

"Yes, but just roll with it for now," Harper whispered back, and then she smiled at Kellan and Blaze both and said, "It's nice to meet you, Blaze."

"He'll be giving us a ride home on their ship. Let's get going," Kellan said.

The four of them walked back to the Autumn Corpse and climbed aboard.

"So, where can we drop you off, mates?" Captain Connors asked.

"Python Cove," Kellan said.

"Python Cove, ay? And what business do you have there?" Captain Connors replied.

"We love their food," Kellan said.

"Ah, yes, they do have good food at their restaurant. Very well. We should get there in about one and a half hours."

Meanwhile, back on the Black Mist, the crew had left Isle of the Ikkakkujuu.

"Where are we heading now? I thought it was Kellan's job to catch up to us," Bruce said.

"Something tells me he'll be at Python Cove. It was our halfway point last time, and regardless, I'm in the mood for some chips and salsa. We have about an hour until we get there. We'll be stopping for three hours max and then heading back to sea. Mr. Nomad, can you please purchase a large supply of chips and salsa from their restaurant so we can have it during our journey back to Sterling Krystalline," Captain Dawson said.

"Aye aye, Captain. Are we trading rum, too?" Mr. Nomad asked.

"Yes, mate, that's the plan," Captain Dawson replied.

The pirates from both the Autumn Corpse and the Black Mist arrived at Python Cove. Harper and Kellan headed to the restaurant after thanking Captain Connors and Blaze for the ride. The crew from the Black Mist headed toward the restaurant, as well, except for Bruce and Barton, who stayed near the ship to sell the rum for cash, and to trade it for other items.

"Are you hungry?" Kellan asked Harper.

"A little. I don't want anything too heavy," Harper replied.

"How about a salad bowl with tofu and some chips and salsa? Maybe a strawberry daiquiri and some lemon waters? We can share everything, and I will make sure everything is in to-go containers. We should be meeting Captain Dawson and the crew here. I did not have another way of getting us here, so I had to convince Blaze to give us a lift. My excuse about food seemed to work," Kellan said.

"Yeah, it definitely worked. I'm ordering tacos," Bryce said.

Once they had ordered and sat down to eat, Kendall and the crew from the Black Mist walked into the restaurant. The pirates placed their orders and headed over to the table where Harper, Bryce, and Kellan were sitting.

"How did you make it back? Glad you're all here," Austin said.

"Boarded the Autumn Corpse," Kellan responded.

"What? But they are an enemy ship," Kendall replied.

"Yes, but do keep in mind that I am still friends with Blaze. I had to disguise myself, and the crew on their ship didn't know who Harper and Bryce were," Kellan said.

"Well, we have news for you, but first let's get back to the Black Mist," Kendall said.

After they had grabbed all of the food they had purchased, and their drinks, the crew walked back to the Black Mist and climbed aboard.

"Ready to go, boys?" Captain Dawson asked Bryce and Barton.

"Aye aye, Captain. We made a profit but still have some rum left," Bruce said.

"Good work. We have tacos for you. You can ask Mr. Nomad for them," Captain Dawson said.

After everyone was aboard the Black Mist, the ship headed toward Sterling Krystalline, and the crew gathered in the captain's quarters to finish eating and to share the news they had with Harper, Bryce, and Kellan.

"So, what's this news you have for us?" Kellan asked as he dipped his chip into some salsa.

"While we were away, we stopped at an island called Isle of the Ikkakkujuu. While we were there, we ran into Kelsey,

Harper's cousin. She was with a group of mermaids who live underneath the island, and the mermaid leader told us about how one of their sisters is currently dating Blaze. Did he mention anything to you?" Kendall asked Kellan.

"He mentioned a girl named Hazel," Kellan replied.

"That's her name. She's been using unicorn dust to turn herself into a human, but she's actually a mermaid. The mermaid leader also told us that there is a legend about a blue necklace that was lost at sea. Apparently, mermaids who once lived on Isle of the Ikkakkujuu hid it, as it was known to have magical powers. The mermaid leader also mentioned that Kelsey's friend Spencer was interested in another pirate in the Autumn Corpse crew," Kendall said.

"So, her point is that we are directly and indirectly tied to the Autumn Corpse crew, although they still do not know who we are due to your constant disguises, Kellan. However, I think that once they see the ship again, they will put two and two together. The second point is that there is more than one item of value in these waters, so keep your eyes open. If anyone should find it, it will alter the reality we live in. Make sure that if you do find it, you let Kendall know so we can see what it is capable of. Kendall has magic that can contain it temporarily," Austin said.

"I didn't think Kelsey was much of an adventurer before now. Maybe we can trust her on our future journeys," Harper said to Bryce.

"It's fine by me. Maybe we can talk to her the next time she comes over for tea, and introduce her properly to the pirates," Bryce said.

"That's a plan," Harper replied.

After the pirates had sailed the ocean for thirty more minutes, the Black Mist at Port Tilbury.

"I believe this is your stop tonight," Kellan said to Harper.

Harper gave Kellan a hug and got off the ship. She and Bryce got into a carriage and were greeted by Spencer, who said, "I hope your journey went well."

"It did. Thank you," Harper replied.

"Am I dropping you both off at the palace tonight?" Spencer asked.

"Yes, please!" Bryce replied.

"You got it," Spencer said.

After a fifteen-minute ride through the city, the two friends arrived at the palace and said goodnight to Spencer after thanking her for the ride. Once inside the palace, they headed upstairs to her room, where they were greeted by Amber.

"I see my parents have spoiled you while I've been gone," Harper said to Amber as she gave her hugs and kisses.

After putting away her backpack, Harper walked over to the window and saw that it was open.

"Bryce, look!" she said.

"Is that supposed to be open?" Bryce asked.

"No, it isn't. Either someone has been here or there is someone inside this room. Check the guest bedroom," Harper said.

Bryce checked the room and did not find anyone inside. He also checked both bathrooms and closets but did not find anyone.

"The coast is clear," he said.

Harper moved closer to the window and looked outside. Kellan was hanging from a rope, and Harper moved back so he could swing into the room.

"What are you doing here? I thought you had left already," Harper said.

"You forgot your sweatshirt on the ship," Kellan replied.

"I'm going to bed. Night, guys," Bryce said, walking off.

"Goodnight," Harper and Kellan replied.

"What's the real reason you came back?" Harper asked Kellan.

"After all that time you spent on the ship with us, I wasn't ready to say goodbye yet," Kellan said.

As the two gazed into each other's eyes, Kellan moved closer to Harper and leaned in. Harper leaned closer, and the two shared a passionate kiss. After their kiss, Kellan said goodnight and climbed out the window, then headed to the Black Mist. Harper watched him leave, waving goodbye, and closed her window.

"Was it awkward this time?" Bryce asked, walking into the room.

"Were you watching us the whole time?" Harper asked him.

"No, but I had a feeling that's what would happen," Bryce said.

Harper smiled. "No, it was never awkward. It felt different this time. I'm taking a shower and heading to bed."

"All right, I'm going to get a water. Be right back," Bryce said.

After Harper had taken a shower and Bryce had gotten some water, both friends said goodnight and went to sleep.

***

When Harper and Bryce woke up the next morning, it was raining outside.

"It's going to be a cold one today," Bryce said.

"My favorite. I can finally wear my new sweatshirt," Harper said.

After they got ready for the day, Harper packed a few items in her backpack and then headed downstairs to grab some tea. Bryce walked into the dining room and played with Amber, and then they both heard a knock at the door. Harper ran past him and opened the door, only to find Kelsey standing in the entryway.

"This is a surprise. Come on in. Where are your parents?" Harper asked.

"They are at home. I need to speak with both of you," Kelsey said.

"We're listening, but before you begin, can I offer you anything to drink? Pumpkin juice, ginger beer, or seltzer?" Harper asked.

"Ginger beer will be fine, thank you," Kelsey replied.

Harper gave Kelsey a ginger beer, and she gave Bryce one, too.

"Okay, so what did you need to tell us?" Bryce asked, gazing into Kelsey's eyes.

"Well, I have been living with my best friend, Spencer, for some time now," Kelsey began.

"You mean our carriage driver?" Harper asked.

"Yes, and we have gone on some adventures together out in the ocean. During those adventures, we met a group of mermaids," Kelsey said.

"Mermaids?" Bryce asked.

"Yes, do you know them?" Kelsey asked.

"Yeah, I think I do," Bryce replied, giving Harper a look.

Harper looked back at him and knew he had a secret he needed to tell her later.

"Anyhow, the mermaids are my friends, and we're in search of a pendant that is said to have magical powers," Kelsey said.

"We've heard of the necklace," Bryce said.

"You have? How?" Kelsey asked.

"We have friends who also know the mermaids and are aware of the necklace you seek," Bryce replied.

"Will you both come with me, then, and help me search for it?" Kelsey said.

"We're in. Let us grab our backpacks, and we'll be off," Harper said.

"Before we go, you should know that I've arranged a ride with pirates," Kelsey said.

"Pirates?" Harper replied.

Harper and Bryce stared at each other, wondering if it would be the crew from the Black Mist.

"The pirates are waiting at Port Tilbury. We'll be taking the carriage there. Come along now," Kelsey said.

After retrieving their backpacks, Harper and Bryce followed Kelsey to the carriage, and the three of them got to the ship that was waiting for them at the port in twenty minutes.

"It was nice seeing all of you. I hope your ride on the Autumn Corpse is equally as smooth," Spencer said as she held the carriage door open.

After she got down, Kelsey walked over to one of the crew members and said, "Hey, Blaze, are we ready to go?"

"Yeah, just about. Who are your friends?" he asked.

"This is Harper, my cousin, and this is Bryce, our friend," Kelsey replied.

"Harper and Bryce? As in Kellan's friends?" Blaze asked.

"Who's Kellan?" Kelsey replied.

"Yes, we're back," Bryce said.

"Well, well ,well, it's good to see familiar faces," Blaze said.

"Likewise," Harper replied.

"Kellan is a friend of mine, a fellow pirate," Blaze said to Kelsey.

"I've yet to meet him, although I'm sure I eventually will," Kelsey replied.

After all four of them had boarded the ship, Blaze introduced them to Keaton, and the five of them started to get to know each other while the ship sailed toward the Isle of the Ikkakkujuu. As the Autumn Corpse got closer to the Isle of the Ikkakkujuu, a thick fog surrounded the ship and the island, making it hard to see. Everything was silent, too silent. Harper began to look around on the ship, and she noticed a black raven that had a purple glow about it sitting on one of the ships sails.

"Bryce, look," Harper said.

"I see it. Are you thinking what I am?" Bryce said.

"Yes, we have to keep an eye on him," Harper replied.

"Okay, that's going to be hard to do considering he's flying away," Bryce said.

"Look, he's headed for the island. We have to see what he's up to," Harper said.

The Autumn Corpse had stopped at the Ikkakkujuu port.

"We will be here for an hour and a half tops," Captain Connors said.

Kelsey got down, and Harper and Bryce followed her.

"Would you both like to meet the mermaids? Or do you prefer to just look for the necklace on the island instead?" Kelsey asked.

"Maybe you can introduce us really quickly before we leave. For now, let's search on the island," Harper said.

The three of them walked to the center of the island and began to look for the necklace.

"Harper!" Bryce said.

"What is it?" Harper said.

"Look, it's the raven! He has the necklace!" Bryce exclaimed.

"He's flying away!" Kelsey said, and she began to throw rocks at him.

"Caw, caw, caw, caw," the raven exclaimed.

"Had you seen the raven before?" Kelsey asked.

"Yes, back on the ship. There is something I need to tell you, Kelsey," Harper said.

"Okay, I'm listening," Kelsey said.

"Do you remember Corbin?" Harper asked.

"Our cousin? What about him?" Kelsey replied.

"Well, he's a warlock, and he has the power to turn into a raven just like the one we saw," Harper said.

"So, you think that was Corbin? That makes sense. But he just got away with the necklace. I don't know why I never thought about looking for it on the island before. The mermaids said it had been hidden by other mermaids, so I never thought they would hide it outside of the water," Kelsey said.

"We will have to hunt him down later, and I'll have to tell Kellan and Kendall about what we saw," Harper said.

"Who are they?" Kelsey asked.

"They are pirates on the ship we sail with occasionally. The Black Mist," Bryce replied.

"The Black Mist? But they are our rivals," Kelsey said.

"I know, but the Autumn Corpse crew doesn't know that yet, and let's make sure it stays that way, at least for now," Bryce said.

"Well, now that Corbin is gone, what should we do? We can't get off this island for another thirty minutes," Kelsey said.

"Let's go meet my family," Bryce replied.

"Your family?" Harper and Kelsey said at the same time.

"Yeah, the mermaids you're talking about are my sisters. Is one of them Pyra or Hazel?" Bryce asked.

"Yes! I met both of them. Wait, so you're a mermaid?" Kelsey asked.

"Yes, I used some magic dust from a shell beneath this part of the sea to turn into a human," Bryce said.

"It's unicorn dust. Hazel used it, too. She's got a thing for Blaze," Kelsey said.

"What?" Bryce exclaimed. "Are they dating?"

"I'm not sure. Maybe you should ask him when we get back to the ship," Kelsey said.

"I think I'll wait for her to tell me," Bryce replied.

When they got to the edge of the water, Kelsey spotted the mermaids sitting on the rocks underneath the unicorn cave.

"Pyra!" Kelsey said, waving.

Pyra waved back as they came closer to her, and she asked, "Bryce? How do you know each other?"

"Bryce is Harper's friend, and I'm her cousin," Kelsey said.

"Oh wow, that's awesome. Well, it is nice to meet you Harper. These are my sisters, and we live underneath this island," Pyra said.

Blaze swam ahead and shouted, "Kelsey, are you guys coming?"

"We'll be right there," Kelsey shouted back.

"We have to go now, but we will be back. I have tons to tell you," Kelsey said to Pyra as they waved goodbye.

The three friends walked back toward the ship, and Bryce looked at Harper and said, "I know. Don't be mad. I never told you because I didn't think it was important at the time."

"It's okay. I am glad we had a chance to meet them before heading back to the Autumn Corpse," Harper replied.

Chapter Eight

Shark Skull Island

Harper and Bryce followed Kelsey back onto the Autumn Corpse, and the ship set sail again.

"Where is our next stop, Blaze?" Kelsey asked.

"An island called Shark Skull Island. We have been using this island to hide rum and other items of value. We trade or sale everything when we stop at Python Cove or other islands. The captain wishes to stop and sell the rum at Python Cove, so we must stop and pick it up. They also have one of the best sushi restaurants in these waters, and the captain likes to get fish and chips sometimes, depending on the type of fish available," Blaze replied.

"You mean shark meat? Gross," Kelsey said.

After the ship had sailed west for an hour, it came to a stop on a shore that had black-and-green sand.

"The sand here is amazing. It's almost as if it has glitter in it," Harper said.

As she looked around, she noticed a green glow and followed it.

"Wait up, Harper," Bryce said, tagging along.

As the glow grew brighter, Harper saw a black sail and said to Bryce, "It's the Black Mist. It's here, but it's hiding."

Harper climbed aboard, and Bryce followed her.

"Hello? Is anyone here?" she said.

Just then, Harper saw the door to the captain's quarters open.

"Harper? What are you doing here?" Kellan said, hugging her.

"I might ask you the same question. We just got off the Autumn Corpse. It's here," Harper said.

"What were you doing aboard their ship?" Kellan asked.

"It's a long story, and we will be happy to share it with you, but maybe at a different time. I think Captain Connors knows we're here now," Bryce said, pointing toward the Autumn Corpse, where the crew was preparing the cannons.

"We stopped on this island to grab some sushi, and because we were in search of more rum, which we did find loads of inside a cave," Kellan said.

"All hands on deck!" Captain Dawson yelled.

"It's time to go. Are you staying with us?" Kellan asked.

"Yes, I'll find a way to let Kelsey know later, but I think it will be obvious," Harper said.

The crew began preparing to fire the cannons after the ship had set sail again. The air was filled with smoke as shots were fired from both ships, and the clouds grew dark and heavy with rain. Rain fell lightly from the sky and began to come down harder as time went on. The pirates had been shooting cannons for over twenty minutes when Harper looked over the edge of the Black Mist.

"We've reached rocks. They could cause the ship to sink," Harper told Bryce.

Bryce looked over the edge himself, verifying what Harper had said, and he saw pointy, silver specks that seemed to be floating in front of them in the water.

"I don't think those are rocks, Harper! They're sharks!" Bryce exclaimed.

"I want a better view," Harper said.

"Be careful," Bryce replied.

Harper leaned over the edge of the ship again, but the rain had begun to pour harder and harder, and she lost her grip on the rope she was holding and fell overboard. When she landed in the water, she panicked and froze, then began to sink deeper and deeper, going down to the bottom of the ocean.

"Kellan! Austin! Harper has fallen off the ship!" Bryce shouted.

Austin and Kellan ran toward the edge of the ship to see if they could find her, and then they grabbed a rope and tossed it overboard.

"I'm jumping in after her," Kellan said, and then he did.

After he landed in the water, Kellan spotted Harper, who was sinking deeper and deeper, and he began to swim after her. Finally, he was able to grab her arms, and once he had both of her arms, he sprinkled the unicorn dust on both her and himself. The dust took effect, and they were both able to breathe underwater. After that, Kellan was able to swim back to shore with her.

The Autumn Corpse had begun to retreat at this point and had started heading in a different direction.

On the boat, Captain Dawson said, "We have to go back for Kellan and Harper. I'm sure they're back on Shark Skull Island by now. Did you give them the dust, Bryce?"

"Yes, I did," he replied.

"We will have to camp out there tonight," Captain Dawson said.

When the Autumn Corpse was finally out of sight, Captain Dawson turned the ship around and quickly headed toward Shark Skull Island. Once the pirates had gotten back to the island, Kendall decided that it would be best if she hid the ship inside of the cave on the left side, as it was a dead end and had green leaves covering the area, almost like curtains. She also opted to stay inside the ship so she could place an invisibility spell on the ship, as well. If any other visitors came to the island, Kendall figured it would be easier to escape with the ship because she would be on it and would be able to lift it into the air with her fairy dust. So, while Kendall and Austin remained on the ship, the rest of the crew got off the ship and ventured into the cave to look for Harper and Kellan. After they had walked deeper into the cave, they spotted them in a corner. They had food and water with them.

"Oh my gosh, thank goodness!" Bryce said, hugging Harper.

"Are you both okay?" Captain Dawson asked.

"Yes, we're fine now. It was a close call. Are we spending the night here?" Kellan asked.

"Yes, we will leave in the morning," Captain Dawson replied.

"Is everyone okay with sleeping on the ship?" Mr. Nomad asked.

"Count us all in! Let's go," Bruce said.

The pirates, Harper, and Bryce all made their way back to the ship, and after boarding they headed to their rooms to sleep.

"I'll keep a weather eye out," Kendall said.

"Thank you," Captain Dawson said.

The pirates slept peacefully all throughout the night, and in the morning Harper was the first one awake. She decided to walk back toward the cave, so she woke Kellan, saying, "Let's go."

"Where are we off to?" Kellan asked.

"I wanted to grab a few seashells for my collection," Harper replied.

As the two walked to the cave and went deeper inside of it, they came across a waterfall.

"It's so beautiful," Harper said, walking under it.

"Are you crazy?" Kellan asked.

"Get underneath it. The water is a bit cold, but it feels really good," Harper said.

"All right," Kellan said, and he stood underneath it. "I'm definitely awake now."

As they were exploring the waterfall, Pyra swam up near a rock and watched them.

"Pyra?" Harper exclaimed, walking over to her. "I wasn't expecting to see you here."

"Sometimes I come here to think. I must be extra careful because of the sharks that surround the island, but aside from that, this place is magical. I love picking the apples from that tree over in the left corner. They're delicious," Pyra said.

As Harper looked over at the apple tree, she noticed a glowing raven sitting on top of the tree.

"Hey, has that raven always been there?" Harper asked Pyra.

"No, I've never seen it before," Pyra said.

"Wait, that is the same raven that Bryce and I saw on the Autumn Corpse. He's got the necklace," Harper said.

"Are you positive?" Kellan asked.

"Yes! He's getting away again," Harper said as Corbin flew away. "We have to go after him."

"We will, but for now let's get back to the Black Mist," Kellan said.

"I'll be back to see you and your sisters soon," Harper said to Pyra.

Pyra waved at both Kellan and Harper, and they made their way back to the ship.

"There you are! We were looking for you! It's time to go," Austin said.

"We have a lead on Corbin! He has the necklace and is headed to Python Cove," Harper said after she had climbed aboard the ship with Kellan.

"How can you be sure? After all, he's a raven. What if he's headed toward Isla Mordaz?" Kendall said.

"You have a point, but if that's the case, there's even more reason to follow him," Kellan said.

"Captain, it seems we have our lead," Austin said.

"Next stop, Python Cove," Captain Dawson said.

***

While the Black Mist headed for Python Cove, Corbin landed on Isla Mordaz and went back to the cave Cosmo was waiting in.

"I'm back, Cosmo. Did you miss me? Those fools think I landed on Python Cove," Corbin said, laughing. He had circled Python Cove twice in order to throw them off. "Now that I have this necklace, I must find a place to hide it before they come after me."

Corbin wanted the necklace in his possession because he wanted something to trade or bargain for the ring with. Although he had heard of the power it held, the necklace was guarded by a binding spell that would not allow Corbin to access its powers. Corbin grabbed the necklace and placed it inside his fanny pack, along with Cosmo, leaving space for him to stick his head out for air. Cosmo coiled himself inside, the necklace underneath him, and Corbin headed toward Ebony Woodlands on foot. It took Corbin a total of an hour and a half to get there, and instead of visiting Clementine and Belinda, he passed their home and entered a part of the woodlands that looked like it had been dimly lit. The lights he saw were coming from fireflies that lived in that part of Ebony Woodlands, and soon he saw fairies wearing aqua clothing. Their makeup was done with different colors, even on the males, and they seemed to sparkle brightly with glitter. Corbin walked until he reached a part of the woodlands that had purple trees and tall mushrooms. As he looked around, he found a spot with blue Chinese wisteria and two lavender amur Japanese maple trees. In the center of the two trees, there was a fairy home that had a window facing the blue Chinese wisteria. The plants made a circle, covering a medium-sized box that sat in the center. Corbin walked up to the box and opened it. To his surprise, the box was empty except for a lock that could be attached to the box. At that moment, he felt someone standing behind him, so he turned around.

"Are you interested in placing something inside this box?" asked a fairy wearing a black dress that was covered with pink glitter.

"Yes, I am. Can you help me with that?" Corbin replied.

"Yes, I can. My name is Elle, and I live inside of the maple tree that is towering above us, along with my husband and our ferret, Jax. There is a window that faces this area, so I will be watching over the box for you," Elle said.

"That sounds perfect. Well, Elle, I will be placing a spell around the box after I place my treasure inside. You must not touch it," Corbin said.

Elle agreed, then walked back into her home and closed the door. She rushed over to the window and looked out to see what Corbin was going to put inside the box.

Corbin looked in his fanny pack, reached inside, and grabbed the necklace. Once he had it in his hands, he looked around to make sure no one else was watching him, then placed the necklace inside the box. He placed a spell on it, and thorns wrapped around the box. he closed the box, locked it, and placed another spell around the outside, creating a pedestal out of marble and turning the wooden box into black stone. Once he knew it was safe, he waved goodbye to Elle and started walking back toward the entrance of Ebony Woodlands with Cosmo.

***

Meanwhile, back at Python Cove, Harper and the pirates had searched far and wide and had not gotten a clue about Corbin's whereabouts.

"He's not here anywhere. There's only one place left to look," Austin said to Harper.

"Isla Mordaz," they both said in unison.

The pirates got aboard the Black Mist and headed for Isla Mordaz once again. While they came up with a plan to cover ground on the island, Mr. Nomad concentrated on cooking their next meal.

"So, how are we going to split up this time?" Austin asked.

"Well, I was thinking that Corbin wouldn't make it obvious, so that rules out the rainforest. However, he could still go to the land of the dinosaurs and hide the necklace there," Kellan said.

"We need to look in places where we haven't gone before, and that leaves Ebony Woodlands, the maple garden near it, and the evergreen mountains," Kendall said. She turned to Bruce and Barton. "Okay, why don't you two and Bryce head into the maple garden? I'll head into the evergreen mountains with Austin. And, Harper, you and Kellan can check Ebony Woodlands."

"Before any of you head out, we will be eating supper. Besides, we have another hour before we arrive," Mr. Nomad said.

The pirates set the table for dinner, and Mr. Nomad grabbed the food.

"What are we having this time?" Bruce asked.

"I made colored stuffers, pirates' blood, and butter delights," Mr. Nomad replied.

"Wow, that sounds amazing. What is in all of it?" Bryce asked.

"Well, the colored stuffers have green, yellow, red, and orange bell peppers on top. The bell peppers are filled with smeared avocados, roasted lemon pepper, tofu in tomato sauce, and pumpkin seeds, and they're topped with banana peppers. The pirates' blood has diet sprite as a base, along with rum extract, melted cinnamon discs, and a dash of cinnamon powder. Hot Tamales float on top, along with whipped cream and Red Hots. Lastly, the butter delights are made with cauliflower bread on the outside, and sun butter, brown sugar, blueberries, and strawberries are mixed together for the inside of the pastry, then baked at three hundred and fifty degrees for thirty minutes. Then they're topped with a drizzle of sugar-free maple syrup," Mr. Nomad said.

"Wow, I can't wait to try it all," Harper said.

"Dig in, everyone. Bon appétit," Mr. Nomad said.

"These colored stuffers are delicious," Austin said.

"Wow, this drink is spicy, like cinnamon spicy, but so good," Bryce said.

"The pastries are so soft. They're just right," Harper said.

"I'm glad you all like the food," Mr. Nomad replied.

The pirates continued to eat their food, and after they had all finished, Bruce and Barton helped Mr. Nomad clear the table, and Harper and Kendall got the captain's table back to its original state.

"We have fifteen minutes until we arrive. Prepare to go ashore," Captain Dawson said.

Everyone chose sturdy things to grab on to. After the Black Mist arrived on the sandy shore of the island, the weather changed from foggy to sunny, but the air remained cold and crisp.

"Does everyone remember how we are splitting up," Austin asked.

"Yes," the pirates replied.

"We will meet back here in three hours. The Black Mist will leave thirty minutes after that time," Captain Dawson said.

"Aye aye, Captain," the crew responded.

While the crew split up and headed to their specific locations, Mr. Nomad stayed on the ship with the captain and helped him get rid of trash and other items they no longer needed on board.

The pirates began to explore the areas they had been assigned to by Kendall, and they searched for clues that would help them find Corbin.

"Over here, guys," Bryce said to Bruce and Barton.

"What did you find, mate?" Bruce and Barton asked.

"It's a cave, and it looks like it was inhabited by someone at some point," Bryce said.

"Look, there's a snakeskin," Barton said.

"Snakeskin? But why would Corbin need that? A spell?" Bryce asked.

"That, or he may or may not have a pet or weird eating habits," Bruce said.

"I'm going to take a sample and show Harper," Bryce said, gathering the snakeskin and placing it inside his backpack after putting it inside a plastic bag. "Let's look in the lake and in between these maple trees."

While they were continuing to search for clues, Kendall and Austin were entering the evergreen mountains.

"These mountains look pretty barren. There are not many places to hide things," Austin said.

"Or so it would seem. Let's search in the dirt. He could have buried the necklace, or we could find a buried clue," Kendall said.

"Good point, but where should we search?" Austin asked.

"Good question. Let's look in the lakes first. We can look near the rocks. We may find a hidden cave. Then we can search near the trees, and lastly, we can check the mountaintops," Kendall said.

"Okay, I'll dive into the lakes. Hold on to my shoes, socks, and towel," Austin said.

"Towel? You brought a towel? What made you pack that in our bag?" Kendall asked.

"I just figured we would need it for a picnic, or if it got too hot. I'll be out soon," Austin replied, diving into the first lake near the mountains.

It took him twenty minutes to circle the lake, and then he got out and said, "I didn't find or see anything out of the ordinary."

"Let's move on to the rocks surrounding the mountains now," Kendall said.

Meanwhile, Kellan and Harper had entered Ebony Woodlands and had just gone past Clementine and Belinda's cottage.

"There are three different paths we can take. Which way do we go?" Kellan asked.

"Something tells me we should go left," Harper replied.

"It's really dark that way. Are you sure?" Kellan asked.

"Yes, I'm sure. Don't tell me you're afraid," Harper said.

"Of course not. Let's go," Kellan said.

As they continued to walk deeper into the left side of the woodlands, Harper saw what seemed to be moving lights appear on both sides of them.

"What are those?" Harper asked, pointing at the lights.

"They look like fireflies," Kellan said.

"They really made this side of the woodlands come to life suddenly. I wonder why they weren't at the beginning of the path," Harper said.

"It may be a defense mechanism against strangers," Kellan said.

They continued to walk farther, and then they stopped when they spotted winged fairies who were all wearing aqua attire that sparkled in the lights of the fireflies.

"They are so beautiful," Harper said.

The fairies stared at Kellan and Harper, and while Kellan looked around for clues, a fairy approached Harper and said, "Hello, you must be new to this part of the woodlands. We rarely get visitors. I'm Elle."

"It's nice to meet you. I'm Harper, and that's Kellan," Harper said, pointing at Kellan.

"How long have you been traveling?" Elle asked.

"Almost an hour and a half now. We are looking for something," Kellan replied.

"What is it that you seek? I'm Will, Elle's husband," Will said as he came up to them.

"Nice to meet you, Will. We are looking for a blue necklace. Has anyone come by with one?" Kellan asked.

"Not that I know of. We must get going. Good luck with your searching. Let's go, hon. Remember that phone call we need to make?" Will said.

"Oh yes, I had almost forgotten. It was nice meeting you both," Elle said.

Elle and Will walked back to their home, shut and locked the door, and pulled down the curtains so that no one could see inside.

"That was strange," Kellan said.

"What do you mean?" Harper asked.

"They rushed off and then closed the door as if they were in danger," Kellan said.

"Maybe they just don't feel comfortable with strangers," Harper said.

They continued to look under rocks and inside trees. Harper walked near Elle's home, wondering why they had rushed off so soon. As she thought about her experience with Elle and Will, she came across several Japanese maples.

"Kellan, come here and look at these trees. I think I may have found something," Harper said.

Kellan walked over to where she was and looked down. He noticed a gray stone and said,

"There is something in the middle of these plants. I'm going to see if I can get inside the circle somehow."

"Let me do it. I'm smaller," Harper said.

"Okay, good point. Wait, look. There is already an entryway on the side that faces Elle's window," Kellan said, walking over to it.

Harper followed Kellan and walked inside of the circle.

"What do you see?" Kellan asked her.

"It's a box. A wooden box, but it is locked," Harper replied.

"Do you know a spell you can cast to open it?" Kellan asked.

"Yes, but I am not one hundred percent sure it will open it," Harper replied.

"Let's try it out before we try to open it by using physical force," Kellan said.

"Okay, here goes nothing. *Wood and stone of hidden secrets, prop yourself open and reveal the danger that lies within. Break the force field's power so I can grab the jewel within this hour,*" Harper said.

The lock then broke, and Harper and Kellan got a glimpse of purple light. When Harper looked inside, she found the blue necklace. She grabbed it and placed it inside her backpack, and the wooden box and stone pedestal disappeared into the ground.

"I can't believe we found it," Harper said, smiling.

"Let's head back now. We have forty minutes left," Kellan said.

The two friends started back in the direction they had come from, but they noticed that the fireflies were no longer there, and the fairies had also gone inside and turned out their lights.

"Something doesn't feel right," Kellan said.

The woodlands had grown pitch-black, and in the distance Kellan saw two sets of eyes glaring back at him, green pixie dust forming a cloud around the figures.

"Oh, you didn't think it would be that easy to take that necklace, did you?" two voices said.

"No, I didn't think so. I hope you have some spells or pixie dust in your bag, Harper," Kellan said, walking closer to the figures. When they were about six inches apart, Kellan could see them both more clearly. "Two witches?" he asked.

"That's right. You didn't think Corbin was going to leave a fairy in charge, did you?" Clementine said, a ball of green fire in her hand.

"Ready to take a shot?" Belinda said to Clementine.

"Ready," Clementine said as she threw the ball of fire toward them.

"Harper, look out," Kellan said.

The witches laughed and continued to take turns shooting balls of green-and-purple fire at them. Harper pulled out some dust and threw it at both witches. When the dust reached them, they froze in their tracks.

"For a minute, I thought we were toast," Kellan said.

"Hurry, let's get out of here before the magic wears off," Harper said, running toward the area where they could exit the woods.

When they reached the area, the woods created a thick bush, blocking their way out.

"What do we do now?" Harper asked.

Kellan tried to use his sword to cut through it, but the bush continued to regrow.

"What else do you have inside your bag? My sword is not working. Try throwing the dust on the bush," Kellan said.

Harper threw the dust at the bush, but this time nothing happened.

"No luck. Try looking for a portal. The witches are coming back this way. The magic didn't last long," Kellan said.

Harper quickly reached into her bag and took out what looked like a black rock, then threw it at the bush. The rock cracked and became a portal with pink swirls.

"Let's go. We have to jump into it. Grab my hand. Ready? Now!" Harper said.

They both jumped into the portal and landed in the meadows of the evergreen forest.

"Are you okay? Where are we?" Kellan said.

"I'm okay. Still have the necklace. Who were those witches? And I am guessing these are the evergreen mountains," Harper said.

"I think you're right. I am not sure about your question. They must have been friends of Corbin's. We better get going. We have ten minutes left on the clock," Kellan said.

The two friends got up and headed toward the open field near the coast of the island. When they got there, the rest of the crew was already waiting there.

"What took you so long? We almost left without you," Austin said.

"Did you find anything?" Kendall asked.

"We were attacked by two witches on our way out," Kellan said.

"We found the necklace. It's in my backpack," Harper said.

"Great work, you two. Hold on to it. You can hand it over when we get back on the Black Mist," Kendall said.

They walked back to the ship, and as they were boarding, the Autumn Corpse arrived. Kendall saw them and quickly cast a spell on the ship and the crew. Once everyone had boarded the Black Mist, she lifted it into the air with her magic dust, and they flew over the cobalt rocks and drifted out over the ocean. Once the ship had landed on the water, she lifted the spell.

"Wow, what happened?" Bryce asked.

"Sorry, I had to put a spell on everything and everyone. Otherwise, the Autumn Corpse crew would have seen us, and I'm sure they would have tried to take the necklace. I still do not know what will happen if the necklace gets into the wrong hands," Kendall replied.

"Well, thanks for bringing us back to safety," Mr. Nomad said.

As the pirates sailed on the sea, heading toward Sterling Krystalline, everyone grew hungry.

"Don't worry, mates. Mr. Nomad has started on dinner, and it will be ready in forty minutes. In the meantime, there are drinks in the captain's quarters. Feel free to help yourselves," Austin said.

The crew headed to the captain's quarters, and Mr. Nomad headed back into the kitchen to finish preparing the food. After they had socialized over ginger beer and seltzers, Mr. Nomad returned.

"What's for dinner tonight?" Bryce asked.

"Pumpkin soup with walnuts and cauliflower bread. There's also imitation butter, sugar-free pumpkin jam, and vegan cheese," Mr. Nomad replied.

"That sounds amazing! I am so excited to try it," Harper said.

After Mr. Nomad had placed the food on the table and everyone had helped themselves, Harper tasted her food and said, "Oh my gosh, this has to be my new favorite food on the entire planet."

"You've outdone yourself, lad. I think the food tastes delicious, and I am not normally a fan of pumpkin," Austin said.

"Thank you both. I am glad you like it," Mr. Nomad said.

Chapter Nine

Isla Ellura

After they had finished eating dinner, everyone helped clean up, and Harper and Kellan headed out onto the ship's front deck. They gazed at the stars as the night grew colder.

"How can we figure out what this necklace does? Is it in a spell book?" Harper asked.

"I think it could be, but it is better to destroy it or hide it for now," Kellan replied.

Meanwhile, Kendall rushed over to the captain and said, "We've got to change course. I have found a place where we can hide the necklace before we drop Harper and Bryce off," and she showed the captain a book full of maps and ocean charts.

"Are you sure? This will add another two days of travel," Captain Dawson said.

"Yes, the quicker it is put away, the better," Kendall said.

"Very well," Captain Dawson replied.

The Black Mist headed east, and most of the crew headed back to the cabins of the ship. As the ship sailed, the weather began to grow colder and colder, and then it grew quiet. The ship came to an abrupt stop, and Harper headed up to the deck to see where they were.

"Why have we stopped?" Harper asked Captain Dawson.

"I had to stop. Otherwise, the ship would have gotten frozen in the ice. You will have to swim or use a spell or magic to get onto the snow-covered mountains," he replied.

Harper looked out and saw the snow and ice that surrounded them, then asked, "Where are we?"

"Isla Ellura," Captain Dawson replied. "It was named Ellura because of its beauty. It often convinces visitors to set foot on the island, but then they're trapped, with no way out, due to heavy weather conditions like blizzards. Plus, the water is so cold that they cannot swim their way off of the island. This is the only place where we have never seen any other people."

"That is why we chose the location. It isn't a place Corbin would frequent," Kendall said as she and the rest of the crew joined them on deck.

"It is pretty cold," Harper said, shivering.

"Let's get you warmed up," Kellan said, handing her a fur coat and a mug full of tea. "You can give Kendall the necklace now. She is going to fly onto the isle and bury it."

Harper took the necklace out of her backpack and gave it to Kellan, and Kellan took it and handed it to Kendall.

"I'll be back. Give me an hour," Kendall said.

Kendall searched the island, flying above it, and she spotted a cave. She landed near the cave and walked inside. As she looked around, she saw a small puddle of water that was in the middle of the walkway. She took the necklace out, dropped it into the puddle, and put a binding spell on it. She covered the puddle with loose snow and then formed a glacier on top of it, closing it off from visitors. Lastly, she placed a protection spell on top of it and then walked back out of the cave. Once she was outside the cave, she flew back to the Black Mist. When she landed, she was out of breath.

"Are you okay? What happened?" Austin asked.

"I flew back as fast as I could. We must leave now! There's a blizzard coming," Kendall said.

Austin ran over to tell Captain Dawson what Kendall had said, then, with Bruce's and Barton's help, began to haul the anchor up. Once the anchor had been raised, the Black Mist headed back south, moving toward Sterling Krystalline.

***

Meanwhile, Corbin had explored Isla Mordaz and had come across the rainforest. He explored it, and when he could not access the treehouse, he decided to cast a spell that revealed its hidden nature, saying aloud, "I know you're hiding in there."

He headed back to his cave and grabbed his crystal ball, then said, "Show me Captain Connors," and the crystal ball showed the Autumn Corpse, Captain Connors steering the ship.

"Time to set this plan in motion, Cosmo," Corbin said.

He put the crystal ball back in its spot inside the cave and took Cosmo with him as he transformed into a raven and flew off the island to search for the Autumn Corpse. Once he spotted the ship, he landed and transformed back into human form.

"Woah, where did you come from?" Keaton asked.

"Isla Mordaz, if you must know. Take me to your captain, please," Corbin replied.

"Sure, follow me," Keaton said, leading him to the captain. "Captain Connors, it seems you have a visitor."

"Well, well, well, it appears I do. What brings you here, Corbin?" Captain Connors asked.

"I have a favor to ask of you," Corbin replied.

"A favor, huh? What is in it for us," Captain Connors replied.

"Well, Harper has found a ring that has powers that one can only dream of. In order to get that ring back from her, we need leverage, and that means mermaids. Bryce has siblings," Corbin said.

"Wait, how do you know Bryce and Harper?" Captain Connors asked.

"Harper is my cousin," Corbin replied.

"I see, and I suppose you want the throne? But that leaves me with nothing," Captain Connors said.

"Yes, but you could be my second in command, and you would have all of the riches you could dream of," Corbin replied.

"Very well. You have a point. We'll take Pyra. Next stop, Isle of the Ikkakkujuu," Captain Connors said as he steered the ship east. "We should be there in an hour tops. Meanwhile, help yourself to some refreshments in my office."

"Thank you, Captain. Don't mind if I do," Corbin replied, grabbing a seltzer and a slice of bread from the baguette in the middle of the table.

***

Back at Port Tilbury, Harper and Bryce had left the Black Mist and gotten into a carriage that was headed for Sterling Krystalline.

"It has been a long journey," Bryce said.

"I don't doubt that there will be an another one soon enough. I'd like to take a shower and get some rest tonight," Harper said.

"Yeah, that sounds relaxing," Bryce replied.

Once they were back at the palace, Harper and Bryce waved goodbye to Spencer and went inside. That night, the two friends slept peacefully.

***

Meanwhile, the pirates had started their journey back toward Skerry Moor, as Captain Dawson planned to see Heidi again. Kendall had agreed to come back for Harper and Bryce after their three-day trip to Skerry Moor. Then they could check the treehouse for the treasures they had hidden. The Black Mist was hidden in the same spot it had been hidden in on their last visit, but before the pirates could go ashore, a mermaid swam up to the ship.

"Help! Please help!" Leah said.

"Leah? What are you doing so far from Isle of the Ikkakkujuu?" Kendall asked.

"They've captured her! She's aboard the Autumn Corpse with Captain Connors and Corbin," Leah replied.

"Who have they captured? Hazel?" Kellan said.

"No! Pyra!" Leah said.

"Pyra? They must need leverage of some sort," Austin said.

"We'll all make haste. For now, go back to your sisters and care for them. We leave in ten minutes. All hands on deck," Captain Dawson said.

Leah swam back toward the Isle of the Ikkakkujuu, and the rest of the crew got back on the Black Mist. Once the ship had arrived at Skerry Moor, Captain Dawson walked to the check-in desk at the inn and grabbed Heidi. When Heidi saw it was Captain Dawson, she grabbed him, and the two made out with each other for a few minutes. Captain Dawson then handed her a note and said, "It says it all. I'll be back. I have to help a friend in need."

Smiling, Heidi waved at him, taking the note in her hand.

After Captain Dawson had boarded the ship, the Black Mist headed toward Python Cove.

"Sorry, mate, that there was little to no time. What makes you think the Autumn Corpse will be at Python Cove?" Austin asked the captain.

"It's all right. At least I got to see her, and she's safe. I figured they would need to stop at some point for food, rum, or things to sell or trade. If they are not there, we will stay the night and head to Shark Skull Island the next day. If they take her to Isla Mordaz, we will have to stop and pick Harper and Bryce up," Captain Dawson replied.

"That's a good plan," Austin said.

The Black Mist arrived at Python Cove an hour and thirty minutes after it had left Skerry Moor, and the captain and his crew were hungry.

"I've taken the liberty of dusting the ship with an invisibility spell. It should buy us eight hours at most," Kendall said.

"Brilliant. Now, can we get some food?" Barton said.

"We can meet at the restaurant, and we will spend an hour there, but keep your eyes open for Pyra and members of the Autumn Corpse. I'm sure they used magic dust to turn her tail into legs," Captain Dawson said.

"Aye aye, Captain," the crew responded.

After the pirates found a table inside the restaurant, they all ordered drinks and food and waited on their waiter to return with their items.

"Have you seen anyone?" Kellan asked Austin.

"No, have you?" Austin replied.

"No. I think Python Cove is an obvious giveaway. Why would Captain Connors come here, especially if Corbin is with him?" Kellan said.

"I think we need to check Shark Skull Island," Kendall said.

"We will rest for two hours here on the island and then head toward Shark Skull Island. Kellan and Austin, you will need to make a plan regarding how we are going to get Pyra back. You're going to need Kendall's help", Captain Dawson said.

"Aye aye, Captain," Austin and Kellan said.

After Captain Dawson said that, the waiter arrived with everyone's orders and drinks, and the pirates enjoyed their meals. Once they had finished eating, the crew checked into their room for the night, and they all took a shower and went to bed. When they woke up the next morning, they realized they had overslept by an hour.

"Woah, we must have been tired. Everyone, get up! Let's get ready to go. You all have twenty minutes," Captain Dawson said.

After the crew had boarded the ship, the Black Mist headed toward Shark Skull Island.

"I hope you two came up with a plan last night," Bruce and Barton said.

"We did. We can't be a hundred percent sure it will work, though," Austin said.

"Well then, I hope you have a plan B," Kendall said.

After sailing for an hour and a half, the Black Mist finally arrived at Shark Skull Island. Kendall cast her invisibility spell on the ship and crew. She also disguised Austin and Kellan before they both ventured out to look for the Autumn Corpse crew inside the cave on the island.

Austin and Kellan hadn't gotten very far when the pirates from the Autumn Corpse came out from hiding and questioned Kellan.

"Well, well, well, who do we have here?" Blaze said.

"My name is Dexter, and this is my friend Sam," Kellan said. "Can you give us a ride home? We seem to be lost."

"How do we know you're not a spy?" Captain Connors asked.

"Well, we don't have a ship on the island, and our raft sank," Austin said.

"Very well. We are to guard this cave. You see, we have been sent here on a mission to capture some mermaids, but they seem to be missing. Do you happen to know where they may have swum off to?" Captain Connors asked.

"Mermaids? I haven't seen any mermaids on this island while I've been here," Kellan replied.

"Who is it who sent you here?" Austin asked.

"His name is Corbin. He needs the mermaids as leverage, or a trade, if you will," Captain Connors replied.

"Why would he need to trade them?" Austin asked.

"He's after a piece of fine jewelry that a young lass named Harper has. Have you heard of her?" Blaze asked.

"I see. No, I haven't, but since the mermaids aren't here, why don't we head to Python Cove, and we can have some drinks? They'll be on us, as payment for passage," Kellan replied.

"I suppose we can do that, seeing as we can't find them anyway. But we will be back.

Vick, you can stay behind with Vince" Captain Connors said.

The crew left the cave, went to the shore, and climbed aboard the Autumn Corpse, along with "Dexter," "Sam," and Pyra. Corbin had used a spell and magic dust to turn her into a human, and the crew had given her some human clothes to wear.

"Welcome aboard the Autumn Corpse, lads. Feel free to roam about," Captain Connors said.

Austin and Kellan walked to the captain's quarters and closed the doors.

"I don't see Corbin anywhere, do you?" Kellan said

"No, he must still be back on the island, looking for Pyra's sisters. Speaking of which, how will we take her back home? Did Kendall give you any magic dust?" Austin said.

"Yes, she did, actually. All we need is to get a moment alone with her, and then we can sprinkle the dust and throw her overboard. She can figure out where to go from there. They won't follow her into the sea," Kellan said.

"All right, it's a plan. Let's wait for the opportune moment," Austin replied.

After Austin and Kellan had a plan to rescue Pyra, they walked onto the front deck, going in different directions. Austin spotted Pyra and initiated a conversation with her, and Kellan walked toward Blaze. He wanted to know how he had ended up on the Autumn Corpse.

"Hey, mate, so how did you end up here, or did you grow up on the Autumn Corpse?" Kellan asked.

"Hey, I was a servant at Sterling Krystalline once. I helped with preparing meals, and I grew up in the manor's corridors. When my parents died of old age, I decided to move out and take an adventure before my next shift at the manor. I was out at the marketplace one night, and I was put in a trance. I couldn't really make out the person who tranced me. He had a purple cloak on. I was knocked unconscious for a few minutes, and after that I woke up on the Autumn Corpse. My clothes had been changed. After that, I just stayed here. I enjoy being a pirate and traveling the seas," Blaze said.

"Princess? How do you know Harper is a princess?" Kellan asked.

"Hazel told me. I was supposed to ask her to be my girlfriend the day our crew captured her sister. I haven't heard from her since," Blaze said.

"Wait. Hazel? She's a mermaid?" Kellan replied.

"Yes, but the captain doesn't know, so I had to pretend I didn't know her when it all happened. Harper is friends with Hazel and Pyra. Now Corbin is trying to find her and take her ring," Blaze said.

"Wow, well, why did you choose to stay with the Autumn Corpse if you knew they were trying to bring Harper and her family down?" Kellan asked.

"I didn't know at first, and by the time I found out, I had already formed relationships with the crew. They're like my family," Blaze said.

"I see. It's a tangled web you've woven for yourself, mate, but you do not have to stay with them," Kellan said.

"What do you mean?" Blaze asked.

"Well, you could always join another crew, travel on a different ship. It's that or be honest with the captain and your crew," Kellan said.

"Yeah, but at what cost? They could easily kick me out of their crew. I don't know what I'd do if that happened," Blaze replied.

"You could join mine," Kellan said.

"Yours?" Blaze asked.

"I'm not alone. My crew, and our ship, is back on Shark Skull Island. It's me. Kellan," Kellan said.

"Oh wow, you mean you tricked me this entire time?" Blaze said louder, taking out his sword to strike Kellan.

"Wait, shhh, someone will hear you, mate. Don't do that. Lower your sword. We need your help to bring the Autumn Corpse crew down, or at least to change their minds about Corbin. I know you don't remember who tranced you, but Pyra can read your memory and tell you who it was," Kellan said, holding up his hands.

"Pyra can do that?" Blaze asked, lowering his sword.

"Yes, help us set her free," Kellan said.

"All right, but I'm only doing this for Hazel," Blaze said.

Kellan and Blaze walked over to where Austin and Pyra were, and Kellan filled Austin and Pyra in on what he had learned from Blaze.

"Can you tell him who tranced him?" Kellan asked Pyra.

"I can try," Pyra said, placing her hands on his head. After a few minutes, she took her hands off and said, "It was Corbin. He was wearing a purple cloak at the time. He's the king's royal advisor."

"Thank you. Now, you better swim until you're deep in the ocean," Blaze said.

"What does he mean?" Pyra asked Austin.

"We're setting you free now," Austin said, and then he grabbed the magic dust, sprinkled it on Pyra, and tossed her into the ocean.

When Pyra landed in the water, her feet changed back into a tail, and she was once again a mermaid. She waved goodbye and dove deep down into the ocean.

"Don't stop swimming," Kellan shouted.

"We better get back to tending the ship. We're almost at Python Cove," Blaze said.

All three of the pirates went back to doing chores aboard the Autumn Corpse until they arrived, and then Captain Conners gave out orders and said to Austin, "We'll be here for an hour tops. I believe you owe us drinks."

"Indeed. I'll order a round at the bar," Austin said, and then they all traveled to the tavern.

After Austin ordered the crew drinks, he and Kellan snuck off to the shore of the island and began to look around.

"There. Kendall must have known leaving was their best option," Austin said.

"There? Where?" Kellan said.

"Follow me. The ship's hidden. Kendall saw me and gave me a signal. Hurry," Austin said.

They both ran over to where the Black Mist was and climbed aboard. Once they were aboard, the ship quickly took off and headed back to Sterling Krystalline.

"We have to pick Harper and Bryce up and head to Isla Mordaz. It's the only place they can't come after us," Captain Dawson said.

***

Meanwhile, back at Python Cove, the pirates from the Autumn Corpse had finished their second round of drinks and were headed toward the ship to leave.

"Where is Pyra?" Captain Conners asked Garret and Lola.

"She was here in the captain's quarters. She must have left when we all left for drinks," Garret said.

"You were supposed to be watching her!" Captain Conners yelled, and then he turned to Lola and asked, "Where are Dexter and Sam?"

"They disappeared after we started drinking. I thought they went for a bathroom run,'" she said

"Ugh! I'm surrounded by amateurs! We have been tricked! They have left the island on another ship, most likely the Black Mist, because I know they couldn't have swum away, not with the sharks in these waters," Captain Connors said.

"Orders, Captain?" Lola asked.

"All aboard the ship! We are going after the Black Mist" Captain Connors said.

The crew climbed aboard the Autumn Corpse, and while they were aboard, Blaze spotted Vick and Vince.

"Hey, how did you get back. I thought you were going to be stuck on Shark Skull Island for a while," Blaze said.

"Well, Corbin ditched us after thirty minutes. He turned into a crow and flew away, giving me some excuse about needing to help the king do something at Sterling Krystalline, so we snuck aboard the Black Mist before they left and was able to climb off the ship when they arrived at Python Cove. Luckily, you hadn't left yet," Vince said.

"Vick! Where is Corbin?" Captain Connors asked, walking over.

"He flew back to Sterling Krystalline, said he had some unfinished business there," Vick said.

"We have our orders, then. How did you manage to get back?" Captain Connors asked.

"Got a lift from the Black Mist," Vick replied.

"So, they were here? And no doubt, they took Dexter and Sam with them, as well," Captain Connors said.

"You've been helpful. It's good to have you back," Lola said.

"Thanks, mate," Vick replied.

The Autumn Corpse then headed toward Sterling Krystalline, in pursuit of the Black Mist, but it would take them an hour and a half to get there.

***

The Black Mist had already arrived at Port Tilbury.

"Go get them, Kellan," Captain Dawson said.

"Aye aye, Captain," Kellan said.

Spencer was waiting nearby, and when she saw the Black Mist, she headed over to pick Kellan up in the carriage. When Kellan arrived at the palace, he knocked on the door.

"Hello, Kellan, come inside. Harper and Bryce are eating dinner inside the dining hall. There is plenty," King Henry said.

"Thank you, sir," Kellan replied, walking over to the dining table and sitting down.

"You're back so soon," Harper said.

"There is chicken, asparagus, and grapes with cheese and crackers, along with cherry-flavored seltzers. Help yourself," Bryce said.

"Thank you, but I can't stay. I'm here to pick you up. Can we take all of this food to go?" Kellan asked.

"Oh, of course! I'll prep it and grab our backpacks while I'm at it," Harper said, leaving the table.

"So, what's up?" Bryce asked Kellan.

"We need your help. Corbin tried to capture your sisters, and we have to get back to Isla Mordaz as soon as possible. He's after the ring," Kellan said.

"What? Oh my gosh! Okay, Harper, we have to go! Are you done?" Bryce exclaimed.

"Yes, coming," Harper replied.

Once Harper was ready, they all said goodbye to Harper's parents and headed out the door, then went to the carriage. Kellan had made sure to let Spencer know he needed her to stick around. Once they were inside the carriage, Spencer drove them back to Port Tilbury, where the Black Mist was waiting for them. After Kellan, Bryce, and Harper arrived at the port, they waved goodbye to Spencer and boarded the ship.

"What do you have there?" Kendall asked Harper.

"Oh, I brought food for everyone," Harper said.

"Let me help you with that," Kendall said as she sprinkled magic dust on the bags of food.

Kendall had the food set up inside the captain's quarters in minutes, and Mr. Nomad took food to Captain Dawson as he steered the ship south.

"Thank you, Harper. It is nice to have a break every now and then," Mr. Nomad said when he came back.

"No problem. I hope you all enjoy it," Harper replied.

After Harper and Bryce had gone and put their bags away, everyone sat down to eat.

"This is really good," Austin said.

"I agree," Kellan replied.

"Us, too," Bruce said.

"Well, I am glad you all liked it," Harper said.

When everyone finished eating, Mr. Nomad cleaned up, and Kellan followed Harper to the captain's room as she flirted with him.

"Did you miss me?" Harper asked.

"Yes, is that even a question?" Kellan replied, pulling Harper closer as they stared into each other's eyes.

They shared multiple kisses, but then Austin knocked on the door and said, "Sorry to interrupt, but have you told her?"

"I was just about to," Kellan replied.

"Sure you were," Austin said, laughing.

"All right, fine, you caught us, but don't tell anyone," Kellan said.

"All right, I won't, but we are thirty minutes away from arriving at Isla Mordaz. I'll get Bryce so we can both fill them in," Austin said.

After Austin had gotten Bryce, they explained what had happened during the time they had been away. Once they were all caught up, the four of them headed out to the front deck and joined the rest of the crew.

"Show me the Autumn Corpse," Kendall said into a small mirror, and the mirror revealed the Autumn Corpse at Port Tilbury. "We have to warn the mermaids not to surface again, or they'll be captured by the Autumn Corpse."

"How will we do that?" Austin asked.

"Bryce, you'll have to send the message. It's in the form of a dust spell. This will let the mermaids know not to rise, at least not until we get back from Isla Mordaz. It has to be you because you're a mermaid, and they speak your language under the sea," Kendall said.

"All right, I'm ready," Bryce replied.

"Okay, here it is. Open the box, and the dust will spill out. Make sure it's all out and hold on to the box until we rise," Kendall said.

"We have arrived, mates. Grab ahold of something. We're going under," Kellan said.

"Good luck, mate," Barton said.

Once the Black Mist had gone underwater, Bryce opened the box and released pink dust and a message for the mermaids. He held on to the box tightly until the ship rose again, now on the shore of Isla Mordaz. As of the pirates gasped for air, and Bryce untied himself from the post and gave Kendall the box.

"Thank you. I'll hold on to this. We are going to need it again on the way back," Kendall said.

"Now that we have arrived, how are we going to split up? Kendall, are you going to place your spell on the Black Mist?" Captain Dawson asked.

"Yes, Captain, the Autumn Corpse crew will know we are here if I don't. I'll get on that now," Kendall said.

"Kendall, you, Austin, and the captain should cover Ebony Woodlands," Kellan said. "Harper, you, Bryce, and I will head to the treehouse. Bruce and Barton, you can cover the evergreen mountains. Mr. Nomad, you can cover the mainland."

"All right, take a hike, lad," Captain Dawson said.

The pirates split up to cover more ground and wait for their enemies.

***

The Autumn Corpse arrived at Port Tilbury shortly after the Black Mist had left.

"Blaze, you and Keaton should go look for Corbin. You have forty minutes. Start at the marketplace, and grab some ginger while you are at it," Captain Connors said.

"Aye aye, Captain," they both replied.

They both hopped off the ship and headed straight into the marketplace. They found the ginger booth and bought two pounds of ginger chews and three pounds of fresh ginger, then stuck everything into their backpacks.

"Do you see Corbin anywhere?" Keaton asked.

"No, I don't," Blaze replied.

"Wait, look there. Do you see the crow?" Keaton said, pointing toward Sterling Krystalline.

"I do. Let's go," Blaze said.

They both began to run over to the crow, and he turned into a human.

"Where have you been? Harper has headed for Isla Mordaz with the Black Mist," Keaton said to Corbin.

"I had things to do for the king. I'm his advisor, remember?" Corbin said.

"Well, let's go. The crew's waiting back at the port," Blaze said.

All three of them walked back to the port and boarded the Autumn Mist.

"It's about time all three of you got here," Captain Connors said.

Once the Autumn Corpse was back at sea, the sky grew darker, and clouds grew heavy with rain as the moon hid its face.

"Rainstorm's a'coming," Vick yelled.

The rain began to fall harder and harder as the crew struggled to keep the ship from turning in the wrong directions.

"If the rain doesn't let up, we will have to stop at an island until the storm passes," Captain Connors said to Lola.

"I'll let the crew know," Lola replied, and after updating the crew, she spotted an island and shouted, "Land ho, straight ahead."

"Good looking out," Captain Connors said.

The pirates prepared to stop at Skerry Moor, and once they arrived, they set off to find food and a place to rest for the night.

Lola walked to the small check-in area at the inn and was greeted by Heidi.

"Hello, welcome to Skerry Moor. How can I help you?" Heidi said.

"I'd like two rooms, some tea and crackers, and dinner, please. There are seven of us total."

"Okay, I have given you two of our larger rooms. They have more beds. Tea will be brought up, along with crackers and the dinner menu. You will have to order from the fairies in your room. Follow me, please," Heidi said, handing Lola the keys.

Lola followed Heidi until they got to the rooms. Lola thanked Heidi, and Heidi walked back to the counter. After she looked at the dinner and tea menus inside the room, Lola placed a large order and headed back to the Autumn Corpse to speak to the captain.

"We're all checked in, Captain, and we have tea, both hot and iced, on the way, along with dinner. Follow me," Lola said.

The captain and the rest of the crew followed Lola to the rooms, and Garret made sure to bring the ginger they had purchased back at the port. Once they were inside the rooms, the pirates headed straight for the showers, but Lola waited for the food.

"Set the ginger up, love" Captain Connors said to Lola.

"Aye aye, Captain," Lola replied.

She prepared the large table inside the room, setting it with the utensils that had already been inside the room. After she set up, there was a knock on the door, and she opened it.

"Your tea, miss," the fairy said, setting it all down on the table.

After that, Lola headed to her room to take a shower before their food arrived. Once everyone was cleaned up, they began to have tea and crackers, talking among themselves. Twenty minutes passed, and then they heard another knock at the door. Lola answered it.

"Your dinner, miss," another fairy said.

"Thank you," Lola said.

The fairy set up the meal on the table and then left.

"Woah, what did you order?" Keaton asked.

"It is definitely really fancy," Blaze said.

"Well, they do not eat meat on this island. Their main source of food is coconuts, so I ordered a coconut salad with brown rice and the sauces they normally top it with, along with roasted banana chips and two different hummus sauces. One is chocolate, and the other is normal hummus," Lola said.

"Wow, it all looks so delicious. It's definitely a change for most of us, a lot healthier," Vince said.

"Yeah, that being said, let's dig in," Vick said.

The pirates helped themselves and began to eat, continuing to interact with each other until they were full and tired. They had managed to finish all of the tea, and Lola placed the leftover rice in a to-go bag. The pirates then headed off to bed and slept for six hours before waking up. When Lola woke up, she heard a knock on the door. When she opened the door, it was another fairy.

"Lake water, tea, and bagel bites?" the fairy asked.

"Oh, what is lake water? I didn't order anything," Lola replied.

"These are on the house. The lake water consists of seltzer water, a lemon wedge, and berries." the fairy replied.

"Oh, okay, thank you, and could you take the dishes, as well?" Lola asked.

"Oh yes, let me grab those for you," the fairy said, picking up the dishes.

"Thank you," Lola said as she shut the door.

"Who was that?" Keaton asked.

"Our breakfast," Lola said.

"You ordered breakfast?" Blaze asked.

"No, it was complimentary," Lola said.

After the rest of the crew woke up and got ready for the day, they all sat down and ate their breakfast.

"Wow, these bagel bites are so good," Vick said.

"Yeah, they are so sweet, and they go perfectly with this tea," Vince replied.

"Sweet? Mine are savory," Vick said.

"They must be all different, then," Lola said.

"All right, lads, you have ten minutes to finish before we head back to the ship," Captain Connors said.

After finishing their breakfast, Lola headed back to the check-in desk to turn in her keys, and the crew and the captain headed back to the Autumn Corpse.

"Here are the keys. Thank you for everything," Lola said to Heidi.

"No problem," Heidi said.

Lola walked back to the ship, and once she had boarded, the Autumn Corpse quickly headed for Isla Mordaz. The storm had passed, and the skies were clear and sunny. But then they arrived at Isla Mordaz, and the weather changed from clear and sunny to clear and gloomy, though there was no sign of rain.

Chapter Ten

The Battle

After the pirates got off the Autumn Corpse, Corbin turned into a crow and flew off, going deeper into the island, heading for the maple garden, and the pirates split up to search for Harper and the ring. Captain Connors went with Lola, and Garret searched the rainforest. Keaton and Vince headed into Ebony Woodlands, and Blaze and Vick searched the evergreen mountains.

When Corbin landed, he headed straight into his cave to feed Cosmo. Once Cosmo had eaten, he put him into a small carrier and headed for Ebony Woodlands. When he arrived, he went straight to Clementine and Belinda's cottage and knocked on the door. When Belinda saw it was him, she opened the door, let him inside, and shut the door again.

"What brings you here? Did you hear about the two visitors in the forest?" Clementine said.

"Yes, I believe part of their crew stole something that belonged to you last time they were here," Belinda said.

"What? You mean...?" Corbin said, trailing off.

"Your necklace is gone," Belinda said.

"We tried to stop them, but they found a portal and escaped," Clementine said.

"You said they're back in Ebony Woodlands?" Corbin asked.

"Yes, well, it isn't the same people, but they are on the same side. I checked my crystal ball," Belinda said.

"I have to go find out why they're here again. Something tells me they have the ring. I will need your help again, but first, can you watch Cosmo for me? I don't want him spending time alone in the cave," Corbin said.

"Oh! You brought him? Let me see him!" Clementine replied.

"Aww, he's adorable," Belinda said. "I'll have the warlock who lives next door watch him if we have to join you in battle."

"I think the two will be the best of friends. He's a young lad named Lennox. He's in his early twenties, I believe," Clementine said.

"All right, that sounds good. I'll put a protective spell on him, as well," Corbin said.

"Very well. Now go find the visitors and give this witch glass a ring if you need us," Belinda said as she walked him out.

Once Corbin had left the witches' cottage, he turned back into a raven and searched for Harper and the crew from the Black Mist.

***

Meanwhile, Harper and Kellan had reached the treehouse, and they went inside, closed all of the windows, and locked both doors.

"Now what? I mean, at some point Corbin and the crew from the Autumn Corpse will come knocking at our doors. Even if they cannot get through, they could cast a curse or spell and take the ring. We must hide or destroy it. Help me think. What's our game plan?" Kellan said.

"I'm thinking," Harper replied.

"It can't be on Isla Ellura because he will find the necklace there, too, and he'd gain unthinkable powers," Kellan said.

"How can we destroy it? It seems indestructible," Harper replied.

"We are going to have to test it and see what works and what doesn't. Whatever you do, don't try it on," Kellan said.

"Oops! It's on my finger now, and it's stuck. It's almost as if it is grabbing ahold of me," Harper said.

"Grabbing ahold of you? Let me see," Kellan replied.

Harper showed Kellan her hand so he could see the ring, and he looked closely at the details.

"Hmm, it seems like it's a spider of some sort. A ceremonial ring that a witch or warlock would use to cast a curse or spell. Maybe that's why it feels like it is grabbing ahold of you," Kellan said.

"A spider? I swear it was a normal ring when I put it on. I love spiders, but I prefer them on the ground, or somewhere other than my finger," Harper said.

"Don't panic. We'll figure out a way to take it off. Now that we have the stuff, let's lock this place up and head toward Ebony Woodlands," Kellan said.

***

Captain Connors, Lola, and Garret had come to a dead end in the rainforest.

"There seems to be a barrier of some sort. It's made for specific creatures. Do you know any spells that can counter this?" Captain Connors asked Lola.

"I'm afraid not, Captain. Even the strongest spell could not break the barrier on this part of the island. It does not seem to have been done by magic. It was set up by the island in order to protect a creature or being from the island. If we were allowed in, we would be able to step through automatically," Lola replied.

"All right, let's head back to the evergreen mountains. We can look there and then head to Ebony Woodlands," Captain Connors said.

***

When Harper and Kellan arrived at Ebony Woodlands, Harper felt an indescribable force preventing her from entering.

"I can't go inside. Something about this ring won't allow it," Harper said.

"That is really strange. Okay, let's head to the evergreen mountains, then, and meet up with the others," Kellan said.

***

Captain Connors, Garret, and Lola arrived at the evergreen mountains and met up with Blaze and Vick.

"Were you lads able to find anything?" the captain asked Blaze and Vick.

"No, not a thing!" Blaze replied.

"Let's meet up with the rest of the crew in Ebony Woodlands," Captain Connors said.

"Aye aye, Captain," the crew replied, leaving the evergreen mountains.

***

Harper and Kellan arrived at the evergreen mountains. When Harper set foot in the land, a number of waves seemed to echo in the air, almost as if to let someone know that they had arrived.

"Can you enter this land?" Kellan asked.

"Yes, I can. Something tells me we should head for the rock mountains," Harper replied.

After walking for about thirty minutes, they ran into Bryce, Bruce, and Barton.

"Hey, did you guys find anything? Or anyone?" Harper asked.

"No, nothing. Just walked for a while. What about you?" Bryce replied.

"No, not yet. I did, however, make the mistake of trying on the ring, and now it won't come off," Harper said.

"Oh boy, that is going to make it really easy for Corbin to find it. We need to figure out how to get it off quickly," Bryce said.

"What's the game plan?" Barton asked.

"We head toward the rock mountains. After we have checked there, we can head back to meet up with the others at Ebony Woodlands," Kellan said.

"Sounds like a good plan to me," Bryce said.

***

The crew from the Autumn Corpse searched for clues inside Ebony Woodlands.

"Where is Corbin? Has anyone seen him yet?" Captain Connors asked.

"No, not yet," Blaze replied.

"Has anyone got a clue where he might be?" Lola asked.

"Look at the path. It looks bright and blue. Let's follow them," Vince said, pointing to a group of crows that were feeding.

"Let's go before they fly away," Keaton said.

When the pirates approached the ravens, all but one flew away.

"Corbin?" Lola asked.

"Caw, caw," the raven said, and then it transformed back into human form.

"Where have you been?" Garret asked.

"Finding what you fools took too long to find," Corbin replied.

"You mean you found Harper?" Vick asked.

"No! I found the ring she supposedly found and took from this island. It was near the witches' cottages," Corbin replied, grinning. "Now I will have control over everything! Ring as glossed as night, grant me the power of ultimate, devilish delight"

"I'm sorry. Is something supposed to happen now? If that was the case, you're out of luck," Lola said.

"I don't understand. This is the ring. It has the gem. Maybe I didn't say the spell right," Corbin said.

"Regardless, why don't we head back to where the witches live and ask one of them if they can take a look at this ring?" Captain Connors said.

"All right, that sounds like a plan," Keaton replied.

The pirates took off with Corbin to find some witches who could help them.

Meanwhile, Captain Dawson, Kendall, and Austin had wandered into a dark alley.

"I do not think we are going the right way at all," Kendall said.

"Me either," Austin replied.

"Maybe we should turn and go back the way we came," Captain Dawson said.

The three friends started walking back the way they came in, but they were greeted by the Autumn Corpse crew.

"Well, well, well, if it isn't half of the crew from the Black Mist," Corbin said.

"How did you know? We were from the Black Mist?" Austin asked.

"I've been watching you," Corbin replied, mischievously grinning.

The pirates from the Autumn Corpse took out their knives, ready to fight, and a battle broke out between them.

"We're outnumbered. We can't take all of them on," Captain Dawson said.

"Blind and bind. Now into the cage to take revenge," Corbin said, casting a spell.

The crew from the Black Mist shrunk in size, and Corbin put them into a small bird cage, locking it so they could not escape.

"What are we going to do now?" Austin asked.

"Don't panic. I'm sure I'll think of something. At least Corbin doesn't have the real ring," Kendall said.

"True. I'm sure Kellan and Harper will have a plan when we run into them," Captain Dawson said.

"Now that we have our prisoners, let's continue heading to the cottages," Captain Connors said.

Once the pirates had reached the cottages, they knocked on Belinda and Clementine's door.

"Who disrupts my slumber?" Belinda asked.

"Corbin and the pirates from the Autumn Corpse," Corbin replied.

"The Autumn Corpse? One moment," Belinda replied.

Inside the cottage, Belinda made sure to clear the place with magic, and she sent Clementine and Cosmo into their yard, transforming it so that the guests could not see they were there. Although she was friends with Corbin, she wasn't sure she could trust the others with him, and she wanted both Clementine and Cosmo to be kept safe. When she had finished, she returned to the front door and opened it, saying, "Come inside."

When the pirates were inside, Belinda grabbed a spell book and placed it on the table.

"Take a seat," she said.

The pirates sat around the table and waited for Belinda to speak as she browsed through the pages of her spell book.

"Now, why have you come to see me? Surely, it is a spell you need in order to vanquish your enemies," Belinda said.

"Actually, we're here to see what you know about a certain ring," Blaze said.

"A ring? If it is the ring I think you're speaking of, it was banished from this island a long time ago," Belinda replied.

"That can't be. Corbin's found it. Show her," Keaton said.

Corbin took the ring out and showed Belinda.

"Did you cast the spell that goes with it?" she asked.

"I did, and nothing happened," Corbin said.

"Let me have it," Belinda said, stretching a hand out for it.

Once Corbin had placed it in her hand, Belinda walked over to the kitchen, grabbed a small cauldron, filled it with water, and placed it on top of the fireplace. Next, she added lavender, crackling green powder, bergamot, pepper, and ginger root. She then lit the cauldron on fire by waving her hand across it. After she had mixed the ingredients, she stirred them with a ladle. When the mixture had begun to boil, she walked toward it and held the ring out, saying, *"Bubble, bubble, toil and trouble. Reveal the gem's true colors. If powers it beholds, unveil it now in all its rubble,"* and then she dropped the ring into the mixture.

Once the ring landed inside the cauldron, the pot began to crack, and the ring was lifted into the air by the green smoke. The pirates gathered near the cauldron, and Belinda put her arms in front of them in case of a chemical reaction. As she stared at the ring, her eyes turned bright blue, and she began to speak, saying, "There are two, one false and one with magical power that could destroy kingdoms depending on whose hands it fell into."

Once she was done speaking, the ring fell back into the cauldron, and fire shot out. Her eyes went back to normal, and she shook her head.

"This ring must be the fake, then. The one meant to trick people into thinking it's the real thing! We must find Harper and take the real ring back from her," Corbin said.

"How will we find her? Is she even on this island?" Lola asked.

"She has to be if half the crew is here," Captain Connors replied.

"Can you help us find her?" Keaton asked Belinda.

"Of course, but first thing's first, where did you find this ring?" Belinda asked Corbin.

"I found it near a creek when I was in the land of the dinosaurs," Corbin replied.

"I see. Location matters. It must have fallen out of Harper's bag or pocket, if that is where she was keeping it, before she found the real ring with powers. I can't give you her exact location, but I can tell you which land she has entered," Belinda said.

"Very well," Blaze said.

Belinda had the pirates sit back at the table, and then she took out her crystal ball and said, "Show me the girl these pirates seek. Whose company does she keep?"

The crystal ball revealed the evergreen mountains.

"So that is where she is! Let's go after her," Corbin said.

The pirates left Belinda's cottage after Corbin thanked her for helping them.

"I'll keep the fake ring as collateral. Good luck!" Belinda said as she waved goodbye to them.

While the pirates headed for the evergreen mountains, Belinda finished making a spell with the potion she had made, and she opened the ring, placing a curse inside of it. She then put the ring on her pointer finger and put the house back to the way it was before the pirates had come to visit.

***

Meanwhile, at the evergreen mountains, Harper and the other half of the Black Mist crew had finally reached the area of the mountains where there was a good chunk of rocks. They were all the same color but were quite different in sizes, and they had grass in between them.

"That is a lot of rocks to dig through," Bruce said.

"Look for openings or clues of some sort. Silly boys, we're not going to dig through all of them," Harper replied.

As the crew began to look for clues, Harper saw something shining on the grass.

"Kellan, look," Harper said.

"Woah, that grass is awfully shiny," Kellan said.

"It's a hidden passage. We must look for an entryway," Harper said as she removed the grass that covered in. When she placed her hand on the copper door, the ring released its clasp and turned into a ring, and she exclaimed, "It becomes the key. This way, guys!"

The pirates followed her as she walked through the passage, and once everyone was inside, it shut automatically and the ring crawled back onto Harper's finger.

"Oh no, I was hoping the ring was only a key. I didn't even feel it crawl back onto my finger," Harper said.

"Hey, the little fellow likes you," Bryce said.

They were now inside of a cave that was brightly lit with candles.

"Where do you think this cave leads?" Barton asked.

"I don't know. Let's find out," Harper replied.

As they walked deeper into the cave, they saw writings on the walls, and there were engraved drawings of spiders. The drawings ranged from one giant drawing of a spider to drawings of a bunch of spiders. They eventually entered what seemed to be the center of the cave. As Harper and the crew looked around, they noticed giant spiderwebs everywhere. The homes that resided inside the cave seemed to be made from wood, and smaller spiderwebs were on the outside of each house.

"Welcome to our home. How may we be of service to you?" said a witch.

She was of average height and was wearing a dark-blue witch's hat that had a blue feather on, along with a fancy black top, sparkly dark-blue leggings, and a pair of sneakers.

"Where are we?" Harper asked.

"We call it Wanderer Palace. Home of the cave spiders," the witch said. "We have a large community of good witches and warlocks here at Wanderer Palace, and we care for the cave spiders. We have four of them that live among us. Well, them and their babies. We make sure they are safe and cared for, and they return the favor. Not very many people are fond of the cave spiders, and the spiders aren't too fond of the sunlight, nor are we, so the living arrangements work out. Anyway, what brings you and your friends here?"

"Well, we were in search of something, or someone, that may be able to tell us anything about this ring," Harper said, lifting her hand to show the witch.

"Where did you get that? I've been searching for this for a very long time. It was stolen by the witches in Ebony Woodlands," the witch replied.

"Stolen? But what does it do?" Harper asked.

"The powers in the gem read the desires of the ring's owner and unleash magic that fulfill those desires. If they are good desires, they can help, but if your intentions are not good and you seek to do evil, the powers will outdo any spell or curse placed by other witches or magic users. Here in Wanderer Palace, this ring is placed in the center of the cave to protect us, and it is guarded by four guards. When we had it, one night, as the guards were taking a break during one of their shifts, Belinda and her friend Clementine stole it, and I had not seen it ever since. We have been very careful about venturing out since that night, because without the ring we face more dangers," the witch said.

"Well, I am glad that you finally have it back. Do you have a name?" Kellan said.

"Oh yes, how silly of me. My name is Blair, and the head warlock here is my husband, Niall," she said. "I can introduce you after we place the ring back in the center of the cave. It will naturally unlock itself from your finger and climb into the wheel. Follow me."

When they walked over to the center of the cave, they saw a rounded, metal wheel. On the front, it had a saying. *True gems will find those who pick cautiously.* And in the center of the wheel, there was an outline of a spider, which was where the ring was meant to go. There was a glass case ready to protect it, and it had a small lock at the bottom.

"We had to fix the glass portion because the other witches broke it last time they were here. It is now enchanted with a spell for added protection," Blair said.

"The saying, what does it mean?" Bryce asked.

"It is something we believe in this community. There are many options, but choosing the correct one will make all the difference in this life," Blair replied.

Suddenly, they heard Corbin behind them, and he said, "Not so fast. You didn't think it would be that easy, did you? I'll take that ring now."

"What makes you think I'm going to just hand it over?" Harper asked.

"Oh, you will! Or your friends will become food for the spiders," Corbin replied, showing them the cage with Kendall, Austin, and Captain Dawson.

"Help!" Austin shouted.

Corbin snapped his fingers, and Austin, Kendall, and Captain Dawson found themselves in the giant spider nests. They were quickly wrapped in their spiderwebs.

"We have to do something," Kellan said to Harper.

"All right, I'll give you the ring, but you have to release my friends, and you can't harm the spiders," Harper said to Corbin.

"Very well. We have an agreement. Now hand it over," Corbin replied, stretching out his hand.

"Have you given any thought to how we will get it back? If you give it to him, he could vanish or cast an immediate spell," Blair said to Harper.

"I have a plan. I'm not sure it will work, but it's worth a try," Harper said.

Harper walked up to Corbin, the ring in her hand, and stared at Kendall. Once Harper had released the ring into Corbin's hand, Kendall was able to get out of the spiderweb. She took out some magic dust and cast a spell. Once she did that, the giant spiders came out onto the web that she was on.

"Now!" Harper said.

Kendall repeated a water spell from memory, which caused buckets of water to appear, and she poured them on Corbin.

"Water? You chose water to try and defeat me?" Corbin said, laughing. "Now you will answer to me." With the ring held up in the sky, Corbin repeated the spell he had previously cast on the false ring. "Now I will have control over everything! *Ring as glossed as night, grant me the power of ultimate, devilish delight.*"

The crew from the Autumn Corpse watched as a light came out of the ring and captured them, putting them in the spider's web.

"Cave spiders, obey me. Go eat your meals now!" Corbin said.

The giant spiders walked over to their webs, drooling as they prepared to eat the crew.

"We were on the same side! Traitor!" Keaton shouted.

"What side? I needed you to find the ring," Corbin replied.

As Blair watched what was happening, she took out a copy of her spell book and began to read a curse.

"Not so fast, dear. You can't defeat me, remember?" Corbin said as he pointed his wand at her, but she pointed her wand back at him.

The powers from both wands fought against each other. Her light was purple, and Corbin's light was orange as it took on the power of the ring.

"Harper, how can we stop him. There has to be a way," Kellan said.

"I know. Follow me," Harper said, running into the production room.

Harper had been observing her surroundings while they had been inside the cave. She called the production room by its name because she assumed that was where people who worked in production did things to help the cave run smoothly. And she was right. The production room was where the witches and wizards made updated parts for their cave. They engraved spider outlines on pieces of gold.

"Why are we here?" Kellan asked.

"We need them to make a replica of the wheel. A small one that's just big enough to trick the ring spider into crawling onto it. If it does, we can take it away from Corbin," Harper said.

"But how will you get close to Corbin? The spiders are controlled by him," Kellan said.

"Go back out and tell Bryce to look for a small spider outside the cave. A black widow or a daddy long legs," Harper said.

"Okay, but I am still confused," Kellan said.

After he had told Bryce what Harper had said, Kellan ran back to the production room, and Bryce took off with Bruce and Barton to find a different kind of spider.

"Can you make a replica of the wheel?" Harper asked the witches and wizards inside the production room.

"We can try. We'll get started right away," one of them responded.

"Great. Can you also increase the size of your parts?" Harper asked.

"As in make them twice the size?"

"Yes, but much bigger. Almost the size of the giant spiders," Harper replied.

"We can try. They may be half the size of them."

"Okay, that is good enough. I'll be back in about five minutes. Have the replica ready," Harper said.

"Okay, we will," another warlock from the production room responded.

"We now need to continue to distract Corbin," Harper said to Kellan.

"Let's have Austin and Captain Dawson throw rocks at him. I'll go tell them," Kellan said.

Once he had given them the message, they both gathered rocks, sticks, and anything they could fire at Corbin, then began to distract him as Blair still fought him with her wand. The ring allowed Corbin to multitask.

At that same moment, Bruce and Barton returned with Bryce. They had a brown widow spider in a jar, and they headed for the production room.

"She's a rarity," Bryce said to Harper.

"Thanks, guys," Harper said, taking the jar, and then she turned to the witches and wizards in the production room. "Okay, can we blow this little guy up as big as he can get?"

"We will try our best. The piece you asked for earlier is ready now," one of them responded.

"Excellent. I'll take that," Harper said, holding onto it. Once the spider had blown up to its maximum size, Harper hopped onto its back and said, "I'm going in. Bryce, give me a portal."

Bryce took a portal out of his bag, and Harper hopped into it with the brown widow spider, appearing close to Corbin. Before he could react, she showed the spider outline she had recreated to the ring spider, and it walked over and got on it. When it saw it was not the actual wheel, it hopped back on Harper's finger and gripped tightly.

"It worked, Kellan," Harper shouted.

"What? No!" Corbin said, falling to the ground after Blair struck him.

"It's my turn now," Harper replied. "Now I will have control over everything! *Ring as glossed as night, grant me the power of ultimate delight, not for evil, but for good. May all of the curses be lifted from victims, understood?*"

After Harper said this, Austin, Kendall, and Captain Dawson went back to their normal sizes, and the cave spiders went back into their nests. The crew members from the Autumn Corpse were also able to get out of the webs that had entangled them.

"After him! He tricked us!" Captain Connors said.

"Aye aye, captain," the crew replied.

"Thanks for showing us the real enemy. I don't think we will have issues moving forward, and don't worry, I'll make Hazel mine, and Keaton will do the same with Spencer when we visit them tonight," Blaze said to Kellan.

"Glad to hear it, mate," Kellan responded, waving.

The pirates from the Autumn Corpse chased Corbin until they had reached their ship.

"Let him go. We'll catch him at some point. For now, let's head to Isle of the Ikkakkujuu," Blaze said.

"Good plan, lad," Captain Connors said.

Back at the cave, Corbin had turned back into a raven and flown back toward Ebony Woodlands to see Cosmo, Clementine, and Belinda.

Harper went back to the production room after everyone had left, and tied the brown widow to the entryway, saying, "Wait here, boy." She said turned to Blair. "How can I shrink him again?"

"Let me help you with that," Blair replied, pointing her wand at the spider and shrinking it back down in size. "Now I'll take the extra gold piece," Blair said, and Harper handed it to her. "Are you ready to put the ring back where it belongs?"

"Yes, let's do it," Harper said.

Harper walked over to the wheel and placed her hand over it. The ring let go of her finger and crawled over to the wheel, placing itself inside the carving.

"Thank you for helping us save our community and these creatures from Corbin. We are forever grateful," Blair said.

"Of course. We will be back to visit, but for now we have to get back to Sterling Krystalline, my family's palace, and warn my father about Corbin. It's a long story," Harper replied.

"All right, good luck," Blair said.

The pirates from the Black Mist headed back through the entryway in the evergreen mountains and started their walk back to the coast of the island.

"We have to warn the king about Corbin before he gets to him," Captain Dawson said.

"Let's hope we make it back in time," Austin said.

***

Meanwhile, Corbin was at Belinda's cottage and was talking to Clementine.

"Did he behave?" Corbin asked her.

"Oh yes. He is so adorable. I can see why you have him as a pet now," Clementine responded.

Corbin got closer to her to take Cosmo, but Clementine placed Cosmo on the floor and pulled Corbin closer, leaning in for a kiss. He leaned in and gave her a kiss, and they continued to kiss until Belinda came into the yard.

"What is all of this? Were you able to steal the ring from Harper?" Belinda asked.

"I had it, but she stole it back and gave it back to Blair. I'm afraid I am also out of a job, as Harper will definitely tell her father. I will have more time to sell items at the marketplace, though. Anything you would like me to sell?" Corbin asked.

"You fool! Blair wins again, for now, but I will plot our revenge. However, your job seems promising," Belinda said.

"I am going to sell the home I bought and buy us a bigger home here in Ebony Woodlands," Corbin said, looking at Clementine. "Will you marry me?"

"Oh, I thought you would never ask. YES!" Clementine said.

Corbin pulled out a ring that had a huge, lavender-colored stone in the middle. There were silver thorns all around it.

"I love it!" Clementine said, smiling.

"That isn't all. I bought you a gift, as well," Corbin said as he looked at Belinda.

"Oh, he is so darling," Belinda said as she picked up the gray-colored kitten he had placed on the floor. "I'm going to name him Oliver."

"Now you will have some company in this place, and I'll help you upgrade it all."

"Well, should we go house hunting, then?" Belinda asked.

"Yes, and then you can help Clementine plan our wedding," Corbin replied.

***

Back on the coast of the island, the pirates had climbed aboard the Black Mist.

"Where to now, Captain?" Austin asked.

"We'll make a stop at Skerry Moor and then head back to Sterling Krystalline," Captain Dawson replied.

"Aye aye, Captain," the crew replied.

After sailing for about an hour and a half, the crew arrived at Skerry Moor. They were hungry and tired.

"We aren't staying this time. I have some food ready to order. Once it is done, I will grab it, and we will be on our way. Mr. Nomad, can you please set up the table inside my quarters and get some drinks going for us?" Captain Dawson said.

"Aye aye, Captain," Mr. Nomad said.

Captain Dawson climbed off the Black Mist and headed for the check-in counter at the inn. When he got to the door, he knocked.

"Come in," a voice said.

Captain Dawson opened the door and saw Heidi at the counter.

"You're back," Heidi said, smiling.

"I had to see you again before heading back to the Sterling Krystalline," Captain Dawson said as he pulled her closer, and they shared a kiss. "Will you do me the honor of marrying me?" he asked, pulling out a ring.

"Oh yes! The ring is beautiful!" Heidi exclaimed, smiling.

Her ring was rose gold. It had a large pink gem, and white diamonds surrounded it.

"I want you to come with me on the ship and join our crew," Captain Dawson said.

"I would love that. You can show me the ropes," Heidi replied.

"Yes, and my crew will help you, as well. Go get your stuff, and I'll place a food order with the food fairies at the inn," Captain Dawson said.

Heidi went and packed up all of her things, and she grabbed some fairy dust to bring along. Captain Dawson went to grab dinner from the inn's market.

"Hello, can I please have nine almond-and-feta salads, along with the coconut cake and a large to-go box of buttery rice and fried plantains," Captain Kyle said to the fairy in charge.

"Of course. There is a ten-minute wait. Is that okay?" the fairy replied.

"Yes, and can I please include that bouquet of pink roses, as well? I want everything in a box and bags," Captain Dawson said, pointing to the roses.

"No problem. Of course," the fairy said.

After ten minutes, Captain Dawson heard his order number and grabbed the items in his order.

"Thank you," he said as he walked back toward the Black Mist.

Once aboard, he gave everything over to Mr. Nomad, Bruce, and Barton.

"I'll be back, lads. If you could also fix up my room, please. We have a guest coming aboard. Harper can switch to the room next to mine. It is a bit smaller, but I am sure she won't mind," Captain Dawson said.

"Aye aye, Captain," they replied.

Mr. Nomad went into the captain's quarters to set up the food and place the roses inside the captain's room. Then he had Bruce and Barton fix and clean up both rooms inside the captain's quarters.

"Harper, you will be switching rooms tonight. I hope that is okay," Mr. Nomad said.

"Of course," Harper replied.

As this was happening, Captain Dawson was walking back toward the check-in counter at the inn, and he grabbed Heidi's bags.

"Ready?" he asked.

"Yes, I left my head fairy, Holly, in charge," Heidi said.

"Awesome. We will come back to visit often," Captain Dawson said.

The two then walked to the Black Mist and climbed aboard.

"Welcome to the Black Mist. Let me take your bags for you," Mr. Nomad said.

Bruce and Barton also helped by taking the bags Captain Dawson was carrying.

"We are about to have dinner inside the captain's quarters. Join us. I'll be sailing the ship tonight," Mr. Nomad said.

"This way," Bruce said.

Once they were all inside, they sat down and began eating, and Mr. Nomad headed for the steering wheel.

"I have some great news. I have asked Heidi here to marry me," Captain Dawson said.

"Congratulations! And great to meet you, Heidi," Harper said, the rest of the crew offered up congratulations.

"Let's dig into this wonderful food. I had to grab a cake so we could celebrate, and there are flowers in your room, darling," Captain Dawson said to Heidi.

"I am honored, and it is a privilege to be a part of this crew and to be your fiancé," Heidi said, smiling.

"Cheers," everyone said.

As the crew enjoyed good food and conversation, the ship sailed smoothly toward Port Tilbury.

***

When they arrived at the port, the weather had changed drastically, and rain began to fall heavily from the sky.

"Austin, tie the ship up and meet us back at Sterling Krystalline," Captain Dawson said.

"Aye aye, Captain," Austin replied.

As the crew rode in a carriage toward the palace, Austin stayed behind to tie the ship up and cover it with a tarp so that the rain would not damage it, as they would be gone a lot longer than usual. Once he had finished, he walked over to the carriage that had come back for him and climbed inside. While he was on his way to the palace, the crew had already gotten there and knocked on the door.

"Harper, honey, oh my, where have you been? You had us worried," her mother said after answering the door. "Are these your friends? Come inside, please."

"Sorry, Mother, we had to stop Corbin from taking over. It is a long story, but Father needs to fire him, or he will try to take over our kingdom," Harper said.

"No need, sweetheart. He called and quit this morning," Harper's mother replied.

"He must have known I'd tell," Harper said to Kellan.

"Yeah, apparently," Kellan said.

"Why don't all of you come into the dining area? We have tea set up," Harper's mother said.

"All right, thank you," Kendall said.

Once they were seated, they began to socialize, and Kellan noticed Kelsey in the other room.

"I'll be right back," he said to Bryce, and then he walked over to Kelsey. "Hey, I didn't know you would be here."

"Hey, I can say the same about you," Kelsey replied.

"Can you keep a secret?" Kellan asked.

"Yes, I can. What's on your mind?" Kelsey replied.

"I am going to ask Harper to marry me. Care to join us in the dining hall? I have one more thing to do before I join you," Kellan said.

"Oh wow, okay, she will be very surprised," Kelsey said, walking toward the dining hall.

When Kellan got back, he found Kelsey talking with Bryce, and he smiled.

"Make your move," he whispered in Bryce's ear.

"Um, Kelsey?" Bryce said.

"Yes?" Kelsey replied.

"I like you very much. Will you be my girlfriend?" Bryce asked nervously.

"Yes!" Kelsey said, grabbing Bryce and stealing a kiss.

The pirates clapped.

"Well, I guess it's my turn now. Harper, you're my best friend and the best thing that could have happened to me. I want to keep going on adventures with you for the rest of my life. Will you marry me?" Kellan asked.

"Kellan, I—" Harper started, but he interrupted her.

"Your father knows. I told him and your mother," he said, holding out a ring.

"Everything?" Harper asked.

"Yes, everything," Kellan replied.

"YES!" Harper said.

Kellan took the ring and placed it on her finger, saying, "You'll be queen now. I was a prince before I was a pirate, but we will get to that later, and we will tell my parents unless your parents beat us to it."

Harper's ring had an aquamarine-colored gem that was surrounded with black diamonds.

Kellan leaned closer and kissed Harper, and everyone cheered.

The pirates, Harper, her family, and Bryce all celebrated that night and stayed up talking. Harper's parents had set up a huge tea bar that had all different flavors of both hot and iced tea, along with lemons, cherries, honey, and sweeteners of every kind.

After everyone had gone to bed, Harper sat outside and looked out at the stars.

"I hope they are all ready for another adventure. Something is telling me that I'll have to go back to Isla Ellura very soon," she said to Amber as she kissed her forehead.

"Caw, caw," a raven that was sitting up on the castle's wall said.

Harper looked up and smiled. She was not scared of her future. There was a change in the winds, and she knew that with every new chapter, the adventure would always be different.

The End

Acknowledgements

An acquaintance I met in college said something to me after one of our writing classes one day, and it stuck like glue. I will never forget it. Those words have been my motivation to keep moving forward with this project during times when I wanted to give up. Thank you for believing in me. This book is also for you.

I would also like to thank my friend who encouraged me to pursue this writing project. You know who you are. Thank you for never standing in my way.

To my parents, thank you for giving me the space and place that I needed in order to achieve this dream. I love you both.

Printed by Libri Plureos GmbH in Hamburg, Germany